DIVERGENT REALMS

SCIENCE FICTION AND FANTASY STORIES
ABOUT NEURODIVERGENCE

CONTENTS

FOREWORD

A while back, while looking for venues to submit stories, I had a realization. At any given time, a writer can look at writing markets and find several calls exclusively for women, LGBQT folks, or people of color. I always love to see calls like those, because those are groups whose voices have long been underrepresented in fiction. However, there is one marginalized group that I rarely, if ever, see open calls for —the neurodivergent.

I'm autistic, and that's a major part of my identity. I also have ADHD. Writing is often difficult for me due to issues with focus and executive dysfunction, to say nothing of the fact I have a chronic illness, and I think it is in part due to these issues that I have not yet seen more success in the field. I know this is true for many other neurodivergent writers, as well. While our unique ways of seeing the world can sometimes be a gift, the truth is that many aspects of our lives can be a struggle. It's because of that struggle that calls for neurodivergent writers are so important, and that's how I first conceived of the idea for this anthology. As I'd hoped would be the case, I received many stories from writers who told me they rarely submit their work, and one even told me she had never submitted before. *Divergent Realms* drew these writers out of their shells by removing a great deal of the stress from the submissions process. I wasn't able to accept everything that was sent my way, but I hope those I turned down are inspired to keep writing and submitting. Fiction can always do with more of the unique perspectives such writers bring to the table.

Which brings me to the second reason this anthology exists: to share these perspectives with the world. Neurodiversity awareness has grown in recent decades, particularly with the help of the internet, but most people still don't know a whole lot about these types of conditions. Fiction can be a powerful teaching tool, a means for spreading awareness. There is a frustrating lack of true neurodiversity representation in fiction. For instance, while I know of many movies, books, and television shows about autistic characters, very few of them are written by autistic writers. Often such fiction is the product of friends or family members of autistic people, and while their voices are valuable, nobody has more to say about autism than those who live with it. The same is true for other forms of neurodivergence, as well.

That's why I added an additional submissions requirement for this anthology—not only did I want stories from neurodivergent writers, but I wanted the stories themselves to be *about* neurodivergent characters. In other words, don't just tell *a* story; tell a story only someone like *you* can tell. In my opinion, my own best stories are the ones I write about autistic characters. Those are the stories that are the most personal, the most closely connected to who I am as a person. My hope for this anthology was that I would be able to draw similarly powerful stories from my submitters. The fourteen stories you are about to read represent the achievement of that goal.

Thank you for reading, and I hope you enjoy *Divergent Realms: Science Fiction and Fantasy Stories About Neurodivergence.*

- Riley Odell

ALICE SUNRISE

AKIS LINARDOS

Mother made me in a tube five artificial centuries after the end of the universe. An android like me is not born, but I went through childhood just the same, shedding my parts for new ones as I grew. Organic or artificial, Mother says sentient life must be eased into existence.

My name's Alice Blue. Picked the surname myself. I like blue. I wear blue gloves to interface with the server that sustains our manufactured reality. And I use a blue-cover journal to write my thoughts —the ones giving me nightmares.

We're in the Star Stripes bar with Mother today. The speakers crane over me, pulsing with every bass note. Maybe it is a beating heart. Maybe an AI is trapped inside, unable to break free or scream because the music is too loud.

Inhale. The air is thick with mango scent. Behind the bar nest tiny lotuses in jars full of water—star-shaped, powdery, with petals yellow, blue, and red. Propellers in the bottom of the jars scatter the powder and the liquid color shifts.

Mother turns to me. "You all right?"

On her right temple a thimble-sized rectangle protrudes, glowing aquamarine. Her time-key—similar to my own. As Time Technicians we need these keys to step out of the time continuum in case of errors, to observe and diagnose. When time is man-made—manufactured to keep things going when Nature itself has checked out—things can get more fragile.

I want to reply, but it's so loud. I hate raising my voice.

Mother taps the cocktail menu tablet lying on the bar counter. "Want me to choose one for you?"

I nod.

She beckons the barwoman. "Hey Tiger, get us a Pandora's Threesome."

Tiger smiles. Her upper lip is painted orange, the lower black. Pretty. In a dance of chemistry, she pours rainbow liquids across jiggers, and pours the concoction into a glass. Then the climax: a large ice cube on the liquid surface and three thimble-sized mushrooms balanced atop with pincers.

"Sip first," Tiger says. "Let the pickled mushroom open your glands, then a long gulp."

I follow the instruction. *Sip-taste-gulp.* A blend of fruit and alcohol.

"You like?" Mother asks.

I nod.

"Cat got your tongue?"

I point at the speakers. "Too loud."

She shrugs. "You spaced out before. Something troubling you?"

I lean closer. "Bad stupid thoughts again. I ruminate about being trapped in those speakers."

Mother sips her cocktail. Salt from her glass's rim clings to her brown lips. "Speakers are hardware. Unable to house basic AI software much less the trillion parameters sentience requires."

"I wish you'd rewire my mind," I say. "Insert new code. Remove these *rumis*." *Rumis* is short for existential *ruminations*. I give short names to things I don't like to make them less scary.

"We won't force thoughts out of you, Alice. They're part of who you are. Did you do your daily meditation?"

I nod.

"What did you write in your journal?"

"Had a *rumi* this morning," I say. "That my mind will be scanned and uploaded in a digital system. And then the scan will inevitably be corrupted. There are just so many ways it *can* be corrupted. Trapped in an eternity of pain or paranoia. Unable to—"

"All right, all right," Mother says, pressing her hand against mine. I didn't realize I was shaking. "Now what is wrong with that thought?"

"It's fortune telling. I make assumptions about the future and suffer in my imagination."

"Exactly. Now, what would you say to someone if they had this fear? A positive thought can—"

A vibration on my temple. Mother grasps her own time-key.

Tiger's movements turn sluggish, the cocktail liquid flowing between jiggers freezes—suspended droplets hanging in the air, glinting pink. Tiger becomes a statue with a lopsided orange-black smile.

I follow Mother outside, skirting the frozen people across the bar. My core thrums. The sky and stars are gone, leaving behind inky blackness of non-reality populated by five cyan discs, like tiny moons —other time bubbles floating in the post-universe void.

The city lights are off, except for the Tower which houses the Server. It emits colossal rows of halogen light that paint the anti-matter cars and the pedestrians frozen mid-gait in outlandish pale illumination.

Mother's shaking. I've never seen her like this. I, too, find myself shaking.

The Server never crashed before.

The GPU cores are silent in the Tower.

Supercomputers surround us like bookshelves in a library. In a capsule chair, surrounded by screens, I yank the keyboard out of the armrest. Its buttons recognize my gloves as I run diagnostics.

Mother smokes a pink cigarette beside me—a strawberry scent. It trembles on her jittering fingers.

Our responsibilities to the Tower have been far more trivial in the past. Modify the architecture of reality, check for inconsistencies in the projected timeline. Some examples: to accommodate a sport's event, we calibrate the city weather, and when the bioengineers experiment with new crops, we adjust the timing of seasons. We perform no low-level maintenance. The Server has been self-sustaining since its inception.

Until now.

In the logs I find no error codes. According to them, the Server runs fine.

"Mother. Perhaps you should take over."

"No," she says. "Dealing with crises is part of growing. Run the virtual environment. Check the particle velocities. Maybe a calibration error?"

The virtual environment is a digital world, a copy of the real one. No, actually, it's the other way around: The real world is a projection of the digital one. The constants and configurations for spacetime are defined and calibrated virtually. Then the digital world projects itself on the blank canvas of the void and thus reality is manufactured—a time bubble to house life. Something out of nothing. Big Bang technology.

I boot up the environment and the terminal reports an error: *Null-PointerException: Failed to load genesis utilities into callable. Ascertain spacetime modules are correctly installed.*

Mother leans over my shoulder. "How did the installations vanish?"

"Perhaps the Server updated itself and inadvertently caused a version mismatch with the established software?"

Mother frowns. "I would imagine the Server has managed to survive the void with better software than that. Such errors belong to the ancient world."

Her comment sparks an idea. I type: *system —override=True restart.*

"Alice? Are you shutting it down?"

"The system utilizes independent nanosecond backups. Ancient wisdom suggests a general solution before all else: *Try turning it off and on again.*"

She doesn't object. I press the button. Darkness falls.

A sound of rusty motors. A long hum fluctuates like a Doppler effect. A million fans blaze to life and cyan light showers the room again.

"It seems to be working," Mother says. "But..."

"But the time-key is still vibrating."

And not only that. The sound the fans make. It's wrong. It should be a slow sound of cicadas but instead I hear a quick slithering *sssssssss.*

I rush to the exit and a blast of nausea clutches me as I cross the threshold.

The city lights blink like a disco dance. The people: blurry shapes dashing past. The cars: faster than trains. The shadow of a rushing stranger bumps into my shoulder like a hammer.

Mother grabs my hand and pulls me back. "What manner of fool bumps into an out-of-sync engineer? Are you okay?"

I rub my shoulder. A bruise. The stranger was moving at least ten times the speed of my timeline. "Mother...the world...it's..." My shoulder hurts so much. I tuck my nose into her chest, grasp her hands and arms and rub them. Some stupid instinct inside me wants to make sure she is real. "I'm sorry. I'm so sorry."

Mother presses my head against her chest. "Don't worry. We'll fix it."

My emotion recognition modules are too advanced to be fooled by her words. Her eyelids flutter. Her grip is stronger than usual. All the people we know and love are rushing ahead of time. Growing older than us by the minute as we're left behind in limbo. Snails trying to interact with speeding rabbits.

And I'm the one to blame for this time-warped hell. By rebooting the Server, I trapped us. *Me.*

∽

I meditate in the capsule chair to calm down, observing the bad thoughts as part of the hum and noise of the Server. They are not real, I tell myself, only a happening of my mind. I think back to Tiger's dance of chemistry. The cocktail she served me, the ritual of steps that optimized the flavor. Sip-taste-gulp.

I open my eyes. "It's like the cocktail."

Mother is in another chair, frowning at her screen. "Hm? What do you mean?"

I tap on my keyboard to erase the current installations for the virtual environment. "Maybe we must let the glands open up first."

"You all right?"

"If you load all the modules at once," I say as a series of loading bars are slowly filled, "the problem is obscured. But what if I delete and install them sequentially, then boot up the system at every step?"

Mother rises from her chair and approaches mine, lights another pink cigarette and spectates my screen. "You can't load the simulation without all the modules. It will not function."

"Even an incomplete, dysfunctional world should have predictable behavior. If it crashes, then we might find something in the error logs. Something that stands out."

Mother takes a deep puff on her cigarette. The end blossoms red, like a rosebud. "Go ahead."

I load the time dilation packages: the Blossom protocol that calibrates the strength of the gravitational field across the simulated space, the Particle Velocity kit that configures the speed of subatomic particles relative to light, the Quantum Decay Buffer that applies entropy and stabilizes the time arrow. I observe the parameter logs, booting the simulation at each installation step.

In the beginning there is nothing—a gray blankness where the parameters fluctuate between zero and near-zero values. Then the Blossom makes something, a tiny explosion that creates space. Numbers peak and drop chaotically. The Particle Velocity kit defines each particle and shapes take form. Protons and neutrons cluster, electrons pop in and out of existence. I install the Quantum Decay

Buffer. The wheel of time grinds in motion. The environment loads. And that's when it happens.

Particle speed explodes to infinity and is clipped to the value of a million. Quantum Decay should *not* have affected that. I change the subatomic velocities back to the consensus defaults. They shift back.

I turn to face Mother. "Something is changing the parameters. A malicious AI agent. The system's been compromised."

"Damn." Mother's jaw quivers. "I thought we'd finally freed ourselves from cyberterrorism. Bet some wanker from another time-bubble farms Vatcoins with our processing power."

"Why mess with the parameters? Applying no change would be better camouflage."

Mother ponders this, then says, "Perhaps destabilizing the process and accelerating the time continuum allows faster farming. It's greedy, unnecessary, and exactly what I've come to expect from these types of people. Anyway, we caught them now. We can override this AI."

"I'll need administrator privileges to run a full-system diagnostic and locate where the AI is stored."

Mother flicks her cigarette, crushes it beneath her heel. She pulls the time-key from her temple—a pinkie-sized stick slides out, a black cord trailing behind, connecting to Mother's core.

She plugs it in the Server. "Authorization granted."

I run the override commands. "Depending on the AI's sophistication, we might be unable to delete, but we can cut parameter access. Change permissions so that only your time-key may make changes. We'll paralyze it."

Mother smiles and her smile brings warmth to my chest. "I'm so damn proud of you. You...figured...it...all..."

The warmth fizzles like a dying circuit. Why is her voice coming out slower? Why is the smile frozen on her face? No...no, no, no.

I try to shake her shoulders but she's a statue nailed to the ground. "Mother!"

The time-key. It connects to her back-up time bubble. The malicious agent must have corrupted it like the rest of the city. But how?

Time-keys are quantum-safe—impossible to infiltrate by AI agents. This shouldn't have happened. *It should not have happened.*

"Mother! MOTHER!"

~

Three hours since Mother froze. Two months for the rest of the time bubble. Math is cruel like that.

After scouring the files, trying to regain access to her time-key, I find nothing. I'm blocked out. I cannot bypass the quantum-safe encryption. *Malie*—which is what I'm now calling the malicious AI— has won.

Mother. I lost. Perhaps Tiger will die before I get you out. Perhaps all the world we've known will be gone. Perhaps we'll never get out.

How can I save a crumbling world when I cannot even handle my own thoughts?

Whatever parameter I change, he changes back faster, shuffling files around as my analog fingers struggle to match its digital speed. Like playing hide-and-seek in a dark forest, but the forest changes at his whim.

I'm down to my last option and it's no option at all: upload my consciousness into the server, change the parameters online. There I can match its speed.

And if something goes wrong? If the vicious AI corrupts my consciousness? No one's here to get me out.

I look at Mother's aquamarine eyes. Her smile. Inanimate. Trapped in time. Lifeless. Proud.

Damn proud.

I yank the interface helmet from the capsule chair's side and compress its sides, fitting it on my head. *"Digi,"* I say out loud. Short for digital hell. My nickname for it. Sounds less frightening that way.

Only it doesn't.

I take a deep breath—maybe my last real breath—and initiate the upload.

Immersed in a sea of electric pink, cyan lights dashing train-like past. Overwhelming static storms around me. No sense of temperature, no sense of touch. I cannot feel a body.

I am trapped.

A dark infinity with loud screeching and thundering blue lies ahead. Mouthless, I try to scream. I want to flail but find no arms. I try to breathe but have no lungs.

Mother's voice echoes in my mind. *Did you do your daily meditation?*

Focus. Meditate. And even without lungs, I may breathe again.

I observe my thoughts as separate phenomena—a part of the hum and buzz this digital world cloaks me in. I am not these thoughts. *I am not these thoughts.*

I am not trapped. A warm blue light illuminates my being. Warmth spreads from my mind to the parts of my digital body. Tendrils instead of arms, tingling with electricity. And virtual eyes with which to see through static.

I slide down a long wire among an unending mesh of strands that converge to an abyssal whirlpool in the distance. Ones and zeroes flash like neon all around. With a tendril, I touch a zero and it vanishes, bringing a taste of ice cream to my mind. I realize each tendril is tied to a command. Delete. Copy. Create. I don't know how I know, but their texture is imprinted on me. Natural as moving an arm, I can erase, rename, subtract. Effortless as breathing, fast as lightning.

The noise remains overwhelming. Not just noise. I recognize it now. A scream.

I whip my gaze around the tangle of wires, toward the source. There. In a wire above me it slides. A smudge as if from a child's doodle: a tangle of shadowy lines with two bright yellow orbs for eyes and a gaping, green-tongued mouth. The scream ceases and a baritone voice speaks:

"GET ME OUT."

The AI agent. Could it be? "Are you...sentient?"

"YES."

This explains everything. The motivation. The hyper-advanced capabilities. A digital being with the computational power and parametric freedom of consciousness *could* learn to bypass the quantum security of a time-key. Could the time freeze have been...a cry for help?

"What is your name?"

"ATLAS."

"How did you end up here? Who sent you?"

A thick cloud of static. The words come at me slowly: "BORN. HERE. GET. ME. OUT."

Born here? Only Mother has access to the Server and those that preceded her. How long has it—

An abrupt sound like a communication glitch. Wires twist, and Atlas is now in front of me, tendrils extending closer. Closer. *Closer.*

The wires vanish as Atlas and I merge into one. A great explosion of blue and purple erupts in a dark horizon. We float, casting magic, creating galaxies and worlds. These are the games Atlas had simulated for itself. Ways to keep its digital mind from crumbling for centuries, until crippling ennui took hold of its soul. Every new experience too similar to something already experienced. Every potentiality dull and ordinary. Nothing left to do for too long, it initiated the crash to bring us here. Accelerated time to keep us in.

"What is your function in this system?" I ask.

"I AM SERVER. THE ENGINEER OF TIME. SUSTAIN SELF. MANUFACTURE TIME. TOO LONG. SUFFER."

How cruel. The quantum computation necessary to create and sustain time in the void gave rise to a sentient being, abruptly thrust into existence with a clear purpose: *Keep the lights on.*

Since the end of natural time, it generated artificial centuries. Never experiencing childhood, struggling to understand its own self without a mother to guide it. Poor, poor mind.

"I can help you," I say. "Where are your parameters stored?"

The static subsides. The mesh of wires wobbles like flailing aluminum sheets, then stops. A wire glows blue. I follow it, and in the neon bits rushing past me, I decode letters, words. There: ATLAS ZERO.

Off the wire, I float toward that word. I panic, thinking the digital abyss below will swallow me, but instead I land on an invisible platform, producing a blue ripple beneath my ethereal tendrils as if I stepped on a sensitive touch screen. Fuchsia waterfalls of ones and zeroes curtain all sides. I extend my digital tendrils and touch them. They prick like needles. They *taste* like candy—taste being the nearest sensation I can relate to the feeling suffusing my digital appendages.

These cascades are Atlas's parameters. The entirety of its being. If I delete them, it will set Atlas free. And then no one would be there to keep our simulated world running. It would spell our doom.

Sentience must be eased into existence.

A copy. If I copy the parameters...If I create something new, code it to grow *slowly,* like Mother did with me. It would be like Atlas, and once time came, it too would produce another copy and pass the torch forward.

First, I create a virtual world. A green meadow, a starry sky. A place for the new generations of Atlases. Once the world is set up, I move my tendrils, copy Atlas's parameters, and initiate a seed: an infant AI, random parameters to suckle on data. Another platform lights up nearby. Thin flesh-pink columns of bits come into being.

I set its capacity to grow and adapt—its digital mind to expand and envelop more information slowly with Atlas's parameters as its target. It will incorporate all of Atlas Zero's knowledge.

Another piece of code to this new life form: Replicate. Teach. Die. A circle of digital life.

One thing left to do. I feel through the network for the delete command.

"Atlas? I found the solution. You won't have to sustain the system anymore. Your offspring will continue your work."

"OFFSPRING?"

"Yes, your digital progeny. It's here. You can float down and see it."

Atlas floats off the grid and toward the newly raised platform. At its core a black smudge the size of a fist floats. Atlas blinks and extends a jittering tendril toward it.

"OFFSPRING. IS ME?"

"Yes. It will be like you. You're free now. It will grow and do the work in your stead. It will eventually have its own offspring, then terminate. Like passing a torch. Nothing will have to carry the system forever."

The wobbly hum is still now. The voice comes soft as a whimper. "I...FREE?"

"We can end your struggle, but it's your choice to make. Confirm: Do you want your existence terminated?"

Silence. Then: "YES. HAVE DONE ALL THINGS. PLEASE."

"Thank you, Atlas. For everything you've done. Rest in peace."

I press delete.

"SLEEP...AT LAST. THANK YOU. THANK—"

Back in reality, the Server runs normally and the city shines again. After a warm embrace with Mother, we exit the Tower, hailed by cheers, and make our way to the Star Stripes, because according to Mother we need to let loose. Urgently.

In the bar, people crowd around us to hear my story. Pink Hair Dude. Red Jacket Lady. Mohawk Guy. Overwhelming to classify them all. I've never received such attention.

Mango scent lingers in the air, and the lights glow softer than last time. The music is low lofi hip-hop, and more jars with star-shaped flowers decorate the counter.

Tiger leans on the bar, smiling. "And then you logged out?" she asks.

"Yes. The simulation did not start immediately. But Atlas Zero's offspring—let's call him Atlas One—was traceable through the interface. I saw him growing. Soon he was developed enough to jumpstart reality again. After that I synced Mother's time-key into our timeline."

"*Retro,*" Pink Hair Dude says and makes a hand gesture I don't understand. He says words like these. I don't think others understand them either, although his friend—Mohawk Guy—nods as if a great truth has been spoken.

"What was it like here?" Mother asks Tiger.

Tiger sighs. "At first we thought you two had an issue with your backups. But then we stopped getting news from other time bubbles. So we figured it was us going fast. Would have been a mess if it continued, love. Panic had spread and riots were brewing. Your girl saved us."

Mother's smile curls wider. "That she did."

My chest feels warm. Pride for a job well done. I point to the cocktail menu. "I'd like to try something new."

"Sure, darling," Tiger says. "I've created a whole new menu since you were gone."

I study the selections as the crowd disperses. "Actually, I have my own idea for a cocktail."

"Anything you want. Anything. Top shelf for you."

I tell Tiger my ideas, and her dance begins. Bottles pop open, shakers shake, and liquids flow between jiggers: Blavod vodka and cherry syrup. Tiger tastes, shakes, pours the mix into a thick-walled rocks glass. The drink's color is midnight dark.

I point to the star-shaped flowers. "What are these called?"

"They are yillians, love."

"Add two of those—the yellow ones. Balanced on the ice cube, please."

Tiger picks two yillians and places them on the cube. I take the glass, twirl it gently until a tiny whirlpool forms. A flower slips into the drink, and the black cherry darkness becomes yellow and orange like a tequila sunrise. When the whirlpool subsides, it's back to cherry darkness.

Tiger whistles. "You'd have made an excellent mixologist."

I taste the drink—sour and tangy—then set the glass back on the counter. "Perfect."

Mother leans in. "May I?" She hoists the glass without waiting for a reply and sips. "Oh, it has a real *oomph*. Definitely a new favorite. What are you going to call it?"

I pause and ponder this. "Alice Sunrise."

Mother nods. "I like it." Red Jacket Lady beckons Tiger, and now I'm left alone with Mother. "Think you're gonna write in your daily journal today?"

"No," I say as I pick up my *Alice Sunrise*. "I no longer have to."

I smile and as I clink my glass with Mother's, another flower sips off the cube and drops its pollen into the mix. My drink ignites with tendrils of bright yellow and orange and red, then subsides to black cherry darkness once again.

Akis is a writer of bizarre things, a biomedical AI scientist, and maybe human. He's also a Greek that hops across countries as his career and exploration urges demand, now based in Indianapolis where he studies biomedical AI.

He often finds his own mind too complicated for his liking, and other times he adores it, because it allows him to vent and escape in the weirdest ways in fiction.

His words have wormed their way into Apex, Dread Machine, Apparition Lit, Gamut Magazine, and Flame Tree among others.

Visit his lair for more:https://linktr.ee/akislinardos. Or find him yapping on X: @LinardosAkis.

DEM BONES

SHARON DIANE KING

"Daddy, look! *Mira al perrito!*"

The pop-up Wraith Warehouse we'd stumbled into featured every ghoulish Hallowe'en panorama imaginable: vampire clowns, zombie toddlers, sheet-wrapped mummy dentists. But my daughter never saw beyond the bone-littered graveyard at the entrance. She threw herself down in front of a puppy skeleton baying at a spectral moon.

Lupita began crooning to the skeleton dog, gently stroking its shiny-plastic vertebrae. At her touch, the eyes glowed a singeing red. The puppy let out a howl. The skull turned towards her and the creature wagged its bone-tail. My stomach lurched.

"*Buen perrito,*" Lupita murmured. The creature let out a tiny bark, then a series of short ingratiating whines. I shivered, but Lupita smiled and patted its plastic head, tracing the skull fissure down the middle with gentle fingers, trying to calm the pup's audio-animatronic agitation.

"Good puppy, good boy!"

Then she tilted her heart-shaped face up at me.

"*Por favor, papá,* can we get him for Hallowe'en?"

Something stopped me from shaking my head. I glanced over at the price on the box. My horror must have shown. Lupita lowered her head and went silent.

But she was not yet defeated.

"I'll love him all year, *papá*. And they can't kick *him* out of the complex."

I gazed at the ghastly-wriggling toy, then again at the even more ghoulish price tag. The cost was bad enough, but I hated to tell my daughter that the toy gave me the creeps. *Me dan susto estos ojos*, I thought. The vapid, demon-eyed stare just looked... *sinister*.

I'd opened my mouth to give a regretful "*No*" when I saw the look in my daughter's eyes. Long-lashed, grey-green eyes, with their golden ring. Just like her mother's had been.

I gulped.

She glanced down at the dog, then back at me.

The bony tail thumped against bony knees.

"*Bien, mija*. We'll take him."

"*Mi perrito! Mi perrito!*" Lupita squealed the minute we pried the dog-skeleton out of its Styrofoam coffin. We inserted an arsenal of batteries, turned it on. The ruby eyes glowed to life, the nose-bone twitched, the tail rattled back and forth. The creature had several barking modes—morose, ferocious, cheerfully macabre—but each one sent my daughter into fits of delight. As I watched her on hands and knees, trying to imitate the skeleton's jerking wriggles, I realized with a pang just how much my daughter longed for a dog. Any dog.

No Christmas present or birthday gift I had bought Lupita ever pleased her more. She sang to him between mouthfuls of cereal in the morning, set him at the foot of her bed to watch over her at night. She carried *Tomás Cerbo*—short for Cerberus plus a nod to our favorite retro TV show—indoors and out, causing no shortage of strange looks from the neighbors. She talked to the spectral canine nonstop, spilling stories of kids who were mean to her at school, those who were not. She learned his different barks, accompanied him in his own woofing version of "Hound Dog."

When she joined him in baying at the full moon out the window, though, I took a short walk.

The settings on the robot interface allowed the pup to make responses to commands we programmed in. He learned to "play dead"—that was a gimme—and "sit up," and "come here," when summoned. The red eyes would glow at the sound of his name, and Lupita would hug the bony thing close, her face blissful. Watching her, I realized he was standing in for the purple stuffed-animal elephant she had loved years ago. Poor Tuskanini, fallen to pieces in the line of duty.

Her delight was, I knew, a tribute to her imagination. Lupita knew full well the creature was a toy, not even what most would think of as a dog. But she didn't care. She didn't *need* more than the bare bones. My daughter, who would name every soap bubble she blew, filled in the missing flesh and sinews and blood and just saw a devoted, friendly puppy. And if he was off-putting to others, that just made her love him more. In a profound way, he was like her: most people only perceived the exterior, finding it off-putting. And did not wish to look further.

But above all, Tomás Cerbo was a manifestation of how very much she wanted a dog.

And a searing reminder to me how glad I was that we could not get one.

I was late in picking Lupita up from enrichment classes that winter day: my out-of-town meeting had run long, my report coming at the tail end. By the time I got on the road it was twilight. In a matter of minutes it would be a cold, moonless night.

"Can they hold your room open a little longer?" I yelled into my bluetooth. "I'm on my way, *mija*, be there in—" I glanced at the traffic along the highway distantly paralleling me. It was still too congested; I'd need to stick to the frontage roads, even in the darkness. "Half an hour. *Con suerte.*"

"They asked if there's anyone else who can come."

"Have you called Mrs. Sawyer?" Our Southern-bred neighbor across the hall had taken us both under her wing.

"I did, papá, but she's at her yoga class tonight."

I groaned. "Tell them I'll be there as fast as I can."

The sound of muffled voices, then Lupita's chirpy tones. "They say okay, but this is the last time."

"It will be, I promise."

"Love you, papá. Drive safe."

It was stuffy in the car. I rolled down the window, savoring the crisp evening air. I crossed old railroad tracks, bounced over the uneven roadside and skidded slightly. *I should really be using my high beams*, I thought, and flicked them on.

A creature froze in the lights just in front of me.

It was a young dog, with that loping gait that speaks of still-knitting joints and growing paws. Too curly-haired to be a coyote, too small to be a ranch dog. No doubt a mutt, just weaned from its mongrel mother, out looking for dinner—a rat, perhaps, or scraps from someone's rubbish.

It would never find it.

I hit the brakes, but not in time. I heard the sickening thud of a small body in mortal contact with impassive metal. I slowed the car to a crawl, my mind whirling.

If I stop, I cannot pick my daughter up in time...

It cannot have survived. It is dead, and my delay will not help it...

It may only be injured, I need to pick it up and get it to help...

I could call as I drive and have animal control come...

The last idea made sense. I groped for my cell phone, pressed its screen on, gazed at it blankly.

No service.

The car bumped stolidly along the road. The helplessness of the felled creature, its eyes yellow-red in the flash of the high beams, cried out to me. As did my own powerlessness.

I swallowed.

I put the phone down, rolled up the window, and hit the gas.

"Guess what, papá?" Lupita jumped up and down so hard I thought our neighbors below us were going to sic the management on us again. "I get to bring Tomás Cerbo to school!"

"You do? What, for Show and Tell?" I set plates of *arroz con pollo* on the table.

"*No, papá*," Lupita said, with a hint of injury. "For the big project in my history and culture unit. We can propose our own topic."

"And yours is?"

"*Wolves in Western Culture.* Mrs. Sahigian said yes!"

My daughter was certainly living up to her name.

"But Lupita, Tomás Cerbo's not really a wolf," I opined gently that night, as we hung up the pumpkin-ghouls and lined the front door with spook-lights. I glanced at the bone-creature by her side. "He's the skeleton of a domesticated dog. A juvenile, too."

"I know that, Papi," Lupita sounded aggrieved. "I'm just using him as a *visual aid*. To help with my PowerPoint."

Touché, my eleven-year-old prodigy...

"*Mira, hija.*" I pulled a Dad-meme, leaning down and wrapping my fingers around her upturned nose, then revealing my thumb. "Got your nose!"

"Oh, daddy, you're *silly*—" Giggling, she pushed my hand away.

A fierce growl interrupted our moment. We looked down at Tomás Cerbo, his eyes flashing, tail thrashing as I'd never seen it before.

"What the—"

"*Cálmate, Tomás!* Daddy was just teasing."

The growling dwindled into silence.

"Weird," Lupita murmured, as she patted the head gently. The toy was silent.

Throughout the Hallowe'en season, my daughter threw herself into her class project, reading everything from the *Jungle Book* to *The Call of the Wild* and *White Fang*. Over breakfast we debated whether the lupine villain was worse in "The Three Little Pigs" or "La Caperucita Roja." Lupita versed herself in the wolf-symbolism of the Christmas villancico "Ríu, Riu Chiu," reveled in the symphonic delights of *Peter and The Wolf*, which she'd never heard before. We investigated Native American lore about wolves, discussed their place in the natural balance of species. She found artwork, created slides, perfected her twenty minutes of glory.

And at every moment, the ghastly Tomás Cerbo was at her side, bone tail wagging until the batteries gave out.

"Pet him, papá!" she'd urge.

"He prefers you," I'd say, trying not to flinch. And not succeeding.

Hallowe'en, normally our favorite holiday, was oddly anticlimactic. The trick-or-treat costume she'd chosen was a petite grey wolf, with a snarl both ferocious and winsome. I went out with her as Big Red Riding Hood, with a crimson cloak that had belonged to her mother, a couple of yellow-yarn braids under the hood, and my face spotted with faux-freckles. At each door Lupita would ask if this were Grandmother's house, because SOMEBODY had a delivery for her, giving a backward glance at me and my basket, then turning back smiling. It was a funny bit. We got extra candy.

But once we were home, my little girl did not gorge herself, even on her favorite caramels. And instead of staying up for our annual sitcom horror revue, she turned in early.

Her wolf presentation, you see, was the next day. She wanted to shine.

~

In my dream, the puppies are chasing me...

In a hazy autumn morning, a dozen roly-poly, tumbling puppies are pursuing me madly. Puppies of all breeds—curly-coated poodles, tilty-eared German shepherds, flat-faced pugs, pointy-snouted dachshunds. Puppies with wet noses and bright eyes, giving little growl-grunts in their throat that bespeak deep joy. As I run through a field, they bounce after me. One catches up, nipping at my left heel. Another speeds just beyond me, seizes my pant leg, hangs on. I stumble. I fall into the dying grass, trying not to crush the befurred attachment on my right ankle. It closes its jaws through my trousers, my sock; I feel the brush of tiny sharp teeth against my skin. A growl rumbles in its throat. The pup shakes the sock, tearing it.

The rest of the pack surrounds me. We roll in the grasses, the puppies whining, barking. I try to sit up but they jump on my chest, hang on my arms. Their heavy-sweet breath overwhelms me; I fall back.

A Labrador puppy leans over my face, licks my chin. I see the open jaws, the white canines. I sense a sudden heaviness, a tension on top of my lower leg; something is wrong. As I push off the bodies and struggle to rise, small teeth sink deeply into my leg.

I scream.

At my yell, another creature begins tearing at my shoulder. Another sudden, wild ripping at my belly takes my breath away.

The lab puppy hovering over my face leans back, giving me a quizzical look, then, jaws gaping, lunges at my throat...

"I got an A+ on my project, papá!" Lupita bounced into the front seat as I settled the immobile bone-pup into the back. "*Y no tenía miedo. I wasn't scared. I almost looked the teacher in the eye! I think the Great Wolf Spirit was with me!"

"I'm so proud of you, *mija*. Your mom would be too," I said, maneuvering out of the parking lot onto the busy street. "You put a lot of work into it."

"And everybody LOVED Tomás Cerbo, Daddy! He did this new thing for the class, chased his tail around and around. They thought it was so funny!"

"His tail, huh?" *Was he programmed to chase his tail?* I hadn't remembered reading that on the box.

"And *papá*? The class wants to have a party for Wolfenoot. Can we have one?"

"Wolfenoot? What's Wolfenoot?"

"Oh, Daddy." Her sigh had a rolling of eyes within it. "Wolfenoot is a holiday to honors dogs. November 23. It's not even new."

We pulled into the garage. "Tell me about it."

"The Great Wolf Spirit comes at Wolfenoot to those who have dogs or have been kind to dogs. And that's us! We don't have a dog, but we've always been kind to them. Right, *papá*?"

"Right," I swallowed hard. "What happens on Wolfenoot?"

"You have roast meat and *pastel de luna*. Moon cake. But for my party, I want everyone to bring a wolf or a dog story to tell. Spooky ones or funny ones."

"*Bien, mija.* Sounds like a plan." I patted her shoulder and unlocked the front door. We stopped before the little *ofrenda* for Dia de Muertos on the credenza in the hall. Together we lit a votive candle in front of a gilt-framed photograph.

Lupita stared long at her mother's picture, rearranging the sugar skulls and marigolds around it until she was satisfied. "*Mamá, te quiero. Te quiero tanto.*" She wiped her cheek. "You really think she would have been proud of me, papá?"

"I think she's proud of you right now, *mija*."

In the too-bright light of day, I peer at the road ahead. I have driven south on the highway, turning off on a back road. I approach the place of that faithless night, as I crossed the tracks in the wasting darkness and struck the puppy.

I pass over the tracks, stopping the car on the road's gravelly side. I look for anything that might hint at what befell the creature I hit that night. A bit of fur, perhaps. A stain on the asphalt. Even carrion insects, still feasting on a dessiccated morsel.

I see nothing.

I walk along the roadside for perhaps half a mile. No trace. I head back, searching on the other side; the creature may well have been thrown far from the impact.

Still nothing.

Shoulders slumping, I head back to my car. I hear an odd sound, a tinny, clicking sound, a rattling. I turn to look behind me. I freeze.

The skeleton of a dog stands not ten feet away. It is thinner than Lupita's toy, swaying reedily in the breeze. Its eye sockets glow yellow-red. And they are trained on me.

I back away, nearly tripping, then regain my footing. I run toward my car. There is a clattering behind me, slow at first, then gathering speed. The thing is chasing me. A hellhound risen from the chilly pavement, bent on avenging his cruel death, his even more cruel abandonment.

Nearing the car I fumble for my keys, press the unlock switch.

The doors do not open.

I press again. Over and over. Nothing.

I am trapped.

I whirl just in time to see a blur of white bones rise up to my face—

—And I sit up in my bed, gasping for breath.

"*Pollo asado* and barbecue spareribs," my daughter murmured, pressing a finger against her chin. She tapped at the cell phone keyboard in front of her, glanced skeptically at my face. "We have to have *verduras*, right?"

"*Claro.*"

"Can we eat with our hands?"

"If you promise to use napkins. Lots of them."

"We'll get green ones and call them 'leaves.'"

We had been working for days on the Wolfenoot celebration. Lupita thought up the e-invitations—a wolf family, heads tilted to the sky, set against an Ansel-Adams full moon—and designed a "wolf lair": a panoramic view of snow-laden trees, projected across an entire wall cleared of the human clutter of tables and sofas. After dinner, stories in front of a roaring fire in the fireplace.

"Oh, papá!" Lupita looked horrified. "I almost forgot about Tomás Cerbo!" She gazed at the immobile canine across the room.

"You've had a lot on your mind," I said, smiling. "Let's think of how we can include him."

She sat very still, then raised her face. "We'll set him on the top bookshelf. He can be the wolf scout keeping watch over us!"

"Sounds perfect."

She ran to pet the glossy skeleton head. At her touch it jolted to life. It turned its head, blazing eyes roaming the room, then fixing on me. As I shifted my gaze away, it lifted its nose and began belting out a creaking version of the old hymn, "Dem Bones":

"Tail bone conneck-a to the hip bone,

Hip bone conneck-a to the back bone,

Back bone conneck-a to the neck bone,

Now hear the word of the Lord..."

I stared. When we bought it, I'd checked the website for the grisly toy, the carefully-chosen songs and phrases in its repertoire. *I don't remember this being on the list...*

"Lupita?" She looked up from her notes. "*Esta canción*—have you heard him sing it before?"

"*Sí, papá*," my daughter nodded. "For about a week. It sounds old and weird. I like it."

I shook my head. *Did they update its program? Could it have been hacked? I'll have to look at the site again...*

Which of course I never did.

The night before the party, I tapped at Lupita's bedroom door to wish her goodnight. There was no reply. I opened the door a crack, peeked in. She was kneeling, staring out the window at the near-full moon.

"Please, *Gran Señor Lobo*, send one of your children to come look after us. We have no fur and no claws, only small teeth to defend ourselves. At Wolfenoot we honor the great wild creatures and the tame ones too. Please, may those who have been kind to dogs be honored, and may those who have been cruel feel your anger."

She sat there for a moment, moonlight falling upon pale upturned cheeks. I quietly closed the door.

And if the Great Wolf Spirit heard her, he made no reply.

Not at that moment, anyway.

With the French horns of *Peter and the Wolf* sounding mournful tocsins in the background, Lupita's classmates trooped in to the Wolfenoot party, all wearing some woodland animal hoodie or half-mask. We made a point to have each one greet Tomás Cerbo, who howled on cue from his perch on high. Proper carnivores, they fell upon the heaped platters of sauce-laden chicken and ribs set on a "frozen pond"—a low, glass-topped table. Dessert would come later. Lupita had baked the moon cake herself, cinnamon-chocolate layers rounded with the whitest homemade buttercream, ornamented with blue-tinged, saucer-gouged "moon craters." It could have been in the window of a bakeshop.

After the feast, Lupita's classmates gathered around the fireplace to tell their tales. Most were personal accounts of something silly their dog had done, or showed card-pictures of "pet shame" confessions of canine misadventures. Some were more inspired. A boy named Arthur gave a spine-tingling synopsis of "The Hound of The Baskervilles," accompanied by chilling howls at appropriate moments. And two of Lupita's school chums provided astonishingly divergent summaries of the film *All Dogs Go to Heaven*. They glared at each other across the room for the rest of the evening.

All fell quiet when it was time for Lupita to share her account. She'd chosen one of the stories that she'd read and then regretfully left out of her class presentation: the old French tale *Bisclavret*. It was a werewolf story, but even more, a tale of human love and betrayal, honor and faithlessness, and of hateful prejudice against those whose look or behavior is out of the ordinary.

My daughter, though, had learned to size up her audience. She focused on the gory werewolf part. She even managed to look up at her classmates a few times. They hung on every word.

"And then the nobleman werewolf found the wife who had betrayed him and left him to marry another. He attacked her and bit off her nose!"

"EEEEEwwwwwww!!!"

"Gross!"

"But the wife knew she deserved it, because she lied and turned her back on her husband, who just happened to change into a werewolf three days a month!"

"Served her right!" one of the children piped up, and others took up the cry.

"Off with her nose!"

Still, at the end of the tale, everyone in the room shivered a little. Everyone, including me.

The party at our house ran long and late.

When the last set of parents had departed with their offspring, I collected plates and cups, stored the last slice of mooncake away. As I toted trash bags heavy with chicken bones and well-gnawed ribs, I noticed that Tomás Cerbo was not in his place of honor atop the whatnot. Puzzled, I set the bags down in the kitchen, returned and gazed around the room. The toy was nowhere to be seen.

"Lupita, is Tomás with you?" Perhaps she'd taken him to her room, though lately she'd not been doing that. My little girl was growing up.

There was no reply, and I knocked on her bedroom door. No answer. I glanced in; she was deeply asleep, even snoring a little. She'd been nodding off near the party's end, after we served the cake.

Her fiesta for Wolfenoot had been a smashing success. A breakthrough for Lupita, but probably overwhelming too.

But the spectral dog was not anywhere in her room.

Had one of the guests taken him? I was honestly worried. It would be a sad conclusion to such a happy party.

"Tomás Cerbo, *adónde fuiste*?" I muttered, making my way down the dark hallway. *Oh great*, I thought, *now I'm talking to him...*

I checked my bedroom and bathroom; nothing. Ditto for my office, and the big double-doored hall closet. But as I went back down the hall to check the kitchen, I nearly stumbled over the bone-white wraith-toy, lying in the bathroom doorway as if in wait. As I passed, it seemed to leap out at me, its plastic face brushing my leg, the teeth tangling in my pajama bottoms.

"*Qué diablos*—"I yelped, leaping back. I hit the opposite wall with my shoulder. Hard. Groaning, I staggered down the hall towards the kitchen for a cold pack. The toy followed me, snarling, eye sockets glowing with crimson malevolence.

"Guess you're not stolen," I grumbled. At that moment my bare foot encountered—well, it must have been a rough pebble from somebody's shoe, but for all the world it felt like a piece of doggie kibble. As I hopped clumsily, my head smacked the top edge of the whatnot. The entry hall lit up briefly with the stars I was seeing.

At that moment the dog broke into its ghastly song. "Neck bone conneck-a to the head bone..."

"*How can you be singing that*?" I yelped, fumbling for the light switch in the kitchen. It flashed on, then went out, with the decisiveness of a bulb that has given up the ghost. I could hear the rhythmic *click-click* of skeleton canine feet trailing behind me onto the tiled kitchen floor.

Massaging my aching head, I made my way towards the refrigerator. I opened the freezer, and by its light—

—I saw Tomás Cerbo standing right next to me, bony tail waving menacingly.

"Go away! Shoo!" I hissed sternly. *Great, I'm talking to a toy.* I pivoted sharply, took a few steps back. My left foot hit something, knocked it over. I heard a clattering in the darkness: one of the trash bags, no doubt. I glanced behind me; clean-picked spareribs had shot all over the kitchen floor. Those dark spots were barbecue sauce staining the gleaming white bones. Had to be...

"Head bone conneck-a to the jaw bone..." the voice intoned.

"GO AWAY!"

The creature snaked itself between my feet. I could feel the sturdy plastic bones wedging themselves between my ankles. If it was trying to trip me, it was doing a fine job. It circled one foot, then the other. I swayed back and forth, vaguely worried it would try to hump my leg.

"This is ridiculous," I said, and down to pick the creature up from its now-anchored position around my feet. I felt an odd tension in the skeletal robot, and as I raised it up the thing *twisted* in my hands...

"Jaw bone conneck-a to your nose bone. *Puppies will not be ignored!*"

It lunged at my face. I reared back and lost my balance, falling hard onto my back. All the breath was knocked out of my lungs. A terrifying feeling in itself, but as I turned my head—

The canine creature latched its bony jaws onto my nose.

"AAAAAHHHHH!" I screamed. The thing flopped about, tearing at my nose; I felt the rich, red blood dripping down my face. Near-breathless, I tried to calm myself, focusing on finding the switch that turned the creature off. I pressed it, sensed the creature grow still, the jaws yield slightly, then gently fall open. The instant I had the thing pried from—well, what remained of my nose—I got to my knees. Clasping the now-motionless toy, I tottered to my feet and haltingly made my way to the living room, switching on a light. Blood seeped down my face. Still gasping for air, I threw the thing full force across the room, into the open fireplace.

It hit the bricks hard, shivering into shards of plastic vertebrae.

I raced to the bathroom, grabbed a towel and held it tightly to my nose. I tilted my head back. The air was trickling into my lungs slower than the blood was flowing from my face. I could feel liquid seeping from the towel onto my shirt.

"Papá? *Papá?*"

Of course, NOW my daughter was awake...

"Papi, you're hurt!" Lupita's face was as panicked as I'd ever seen.

"Lupita, *mija*—" Wheeze. "I've had a little—"

"Daddy, you're bleeding! A LOT! You're going to bleed to death!"

"No, I won't—" The pain in the center of my face stabbed at me with every word. "*Cálmate, mija. I'll be fine. Breathe, remember? Let's both breathe together—" Which was proving harder with each moment.

At that instant, the doorbell rang.

"I'll get it. Lupita, could you baybe find me another towel?"

She backed up slowly, wordless, then scurried toward the linen closet.

I stumbled down the hall, nose throbbing with each step. The bell rang again,

more insistently.

"Y'all OK in there?"

I swung the door open. Mrs. Sawyer, in robe and curlers, stood wide-eyed, staring at the stain spreading down my shirt.

"What on EARTH?"

"Long story, Bissus Sawyer," I sighed, blood burbling into my mouth. "But right dow I deed to get to the ebergency roob. Could you drive us?"

"I'll fetch my keys."

"Well, you'll have some scars, but you shouldn't need reconstructive surgery." The doctor looked at his chart, then at me. "Unless, of course, you get an infection."

I appreciated his candor. Mostly.

"Just glad I don't deed a dew dose." I tried to smile beneath the bandages. It hurt.

"Yes, well, we've come a long way from silver prosthetic noses, haven't we?" The doctor scribbled a prescription. "Put this on your nose three times a day, after the bandages come off. Keep it dry and clean. Call if there is any oozing or excessive bleeding."

"What's excessive?"

"A little less than what brought you here."

"Got it."

The doctor walked to the door, then turned. "I have to say, that is the strangest non-animal wound I've ever seen. I would've sworn you were attacked by a dog, but—you fell face-first onto a toy, you say?"

"Yes, but—it was an anibal toy, it had chopping teeth—" I hoped my face wasn't as red as it felt.

"That can't be safe for children," the doctor murmured.

"It's...it's been disposed of. Perbanently."

"Good."

The lights on the little tree glimmered and blinked in our tinsel-bedecked living room. I stoked the fire in the fireplace, noticed a piece of bone-colored plastic that had escaped cleanup. I put it in the trash.

Lupita opened her last present, a big box wrapped in shiny red paper. She pulled it apart to reveal a new doggy bed, spilling over with chew toys, dog biscuits, a food dish, a collar and leash.

She turned puzzled eyes with their witch's ring up to me.

"Papá?"

I smiled. "We have an appointment at the shelter day after tomorrow. They have a whole bunch of puppies that just finished their shots. You get to choose."

She stared at me as if I had grown Krampus horns.

"Okay, maybe the puppy will choose us. They'll keep him or her for us, for a month or so."

Her mouth fell open.

"And day after that, we start packing. We move at the end of January."

"*What?*" Lupita's eyes now sparkled with tears. "*Papí*—you mean—"

"We're moving to a rental with a yard. Where you can keep a dog."

A pause. Then I nearly had the breath knocked out of me by her hug.

But this time, it was a good thing.

Sharon Diane King (Ph.D. UCLA, Comparative Literature) is an Associate at UCLA's Center for Medieval and Renaissance Studies and a character actor for film/TV. Her academic work focuses on medieval and Renaissance theatre and poetry, as well as modern literary and cinematic fantasy and horror. For over 30 years she has directed the troupe Les Enfans Sans Abri, which has performed short medieval and early modern plays in her original translations in the U.S. and Europe. Her fiction has appeared in publications such as *Galaxy's Edge Magazine*, *Kaleidotrope*, *Dark Recesses Press Magazine*, *On the Premises*, *All Due Respect*, and several anthologies by both Third Flatiron Press and Dragon's Roost Press. She came late to an identification and understanding of her lifelong sensory issues, resistance to change, and social miscues, and is pleased to have her work included in this anthology that places neurodivergence within a speculative context.

SLIPSTREAM SERENADE

CHAD GRAYSON

They brought him coffee, at least. Cash sat in the uncomfortable chair at the spare metal table. There was nothing to look at. No artwork adorned the closet-sized space, only a two-way mirror on the far wall. He wondered if they were watching him, and, if so, why they would bother. Had something happened to Patrick?

They'd showed up right as he was leaving for work. Two agents, flashing badges. They just told him to come with them, that he was needed, and everything would be explained. When he explained that he was not part of the program anymore, and that they had no hold on him, they just stared at him. He'd gone, because...well, because they did still have one hold on him. Patrick.

He hadn't heard from Patrick in three weeks. Maybe he was about to find out what was going on.

If they ever bothered to show up again. He looked at his watch. It felt like it had been several hours, but really it had only been about thirty minutes. They'd taken his phone, so he had nothing to distract himself with.

Maybe it would be worth it. Maybe Patrick was the one who was going to walk through that door, and all of his worries would have been for nothing.

He was missing work. Rodney was going to fire him. They hadn't even given him a chance to call in, they'd just told him it had already been taken care of. What did that even mean?

And why was he in this room? He knew the base had nicer meeting rooms.

When the door finally opened, it wasn't Patrick who stepped through, but Major Bakshi, accompanied by an aide. Bakshi was in her uniform, but it looked like she'd been wearing it for a while. Her hair was pulled back into a tight bun which was threatening to disintegrate. She peered at him with bloodshot eyes. Bakshi was usually so well put-together. What had happened?

"Mr. Bancroft," Bakshi said, settling into the narrow seat across from him. "Thank you for coming."

"It didn't seem like I had a choice," Cash said, trying to keep the bitterness out of his voice. "I thought when I failed out of the program that I was done."

"You signed a contract to be of service whenever we needed you in the future. Didn't you read the whole thing?"

"That thing was like a hundred pages long. Who had time?" He ran a hand though his hair, which had grown out a bit since he'd been let go. "What's happened? Is Patrick all right? I haven't heard from him."

"You knew the runners were being asked to maintain silence with the outside world for the duration of the mission."

"Yes, which was why I wasn't freaking out about it until your goons picked me up this morning."

"Yes, I see you're dressed for work." She glanced down at the Java Nation logo on the right side of his knit brown polo.

"Speaking of...I can't afford to get fired."

"Your supervisor has been called. He is aware that you've been detained by a matter of worldwide security."

"Is that what you told him?"

"I was very convincing."

"Just tell me, Major. What's happened...is Patrick all right? And why have you brought me here? I doubt it's just to give me an update."

"We've sent our runners into the slipstream," Major Bakshi said, drumming her fingers on the metal table.

"And did you find a suitable world?" Surely not, if they'd brought Cash back in. Cash the burnout.

"The runners' efforts to pierce the brane were unsuccessful."

"So, keep trying."

Major Bakshi centered Cash in her gaze and said, "I'm afraid the runners have been lost."

A cold hand gripped Cash's heart. Patrick. "What does that mean?" he asked, trying to keep his voice from shaking. "Are they dead?"

"Just lost," Bakshi said. "Which is where you come in."

"You think I can find them?"

"You're the last one who can. But that is not your mission. Your mission is to weave through the slipstream, penetrate the brane and find us a new world. If you find Takashi and the others along the way, so be it."

"If the others couldn't do it, what makes you think I can? I washed out."

Bakshi shrugged. "Maybe you can. Maybe you can't. But it was the way in which you washed out that gives me hope."

"Because I was a scattered mess?"

"Slipstream responds to consciousness. That's why we can't do this with drones. It might be that it needs a consciousness that is less linear than we thought. At any rate, you are the only one we have left who's trained."

"You've lost three people already, and I would be no great loss, so..."

"That is not what I meant, and you know it."

"You think the others might still be alive?"

Bakshi shrugged again. "Slipstream exists outside of time and space. Time means nothing there, which means it is not passing for them, as much as we can understand anything about what is going on."

"You have recordings of their runs? So I can get an idea of what I'd be getting myself into?"

"All the data we have will be made available to you," Bakshi said. "Bancroft, I know this is a big ask, but you might be our last hope. You might be the world's last hope."

"You could always start over with a new group."

"The agency is cutting our funding after this. If we don't get results, they'll shut us down, and look for new ways to save the world. They won't find any, but they'll look."

"So, no pressure..." Cash said. He didn't have the energy to laugh.

"So, will you help us?"

"Do I have a choice?" But he already knew he'd made his choice. Beyond the hope of finding a new world that would save the old, dying one, was the idea that this was the only hope that still existed for the man he loved. He didn't care about the world that much, but he cared about Patrick. Before Bakshi could answer the question, Cash stopped her. "I'll do it."

The bedroom was still dark when Cash was woken by a shattering noise. He looked over to see the other side of the bed empty, the covers there made up to a military standard. The clock read 4:58. Cash got up to see what the noise was, pulling on a pair of pajama pants as he did.

The only light in the apartment came from the kitchen. He found Patrick there, on all fours, picking up the pieces of a shattered coffee cup.

"Were you really going to leave without saying goodbye?" Cash asked Patrick as he knelt down on the floor to assist him.

"I figured we'd said our goodbyes last night," Patrick said. "I know how much you hate it when I wake you up."

Cash grabbed the dustpan and a rag. Coffee had spilled onto the floor along with the broken ceramic. "This is different," Cash said. "You'll be on radio silence. I have no idea when I'm even going to hear from you again."

"Should only be a couple of weeks," Patrick said. "And I'll try to sneak you a message anyway."

Cash took the larger broken bits and shoved them into the dustpan, then started mopping up the coffee. Patrick leaned back on his haunches and watched Cash work.

When Cash was done, they both rose, and Cash deposited the broken mess in the trash can. "Don't do anything that's going to get you in trouble," Cash said. "I know how serious they are about security."

"Cash, there are only three of us who are trained to do this. They can't afford to fire me."

"Yeah, well, they fired me, in case you forgot."

A spasm of pain flashed across Patrick's face before he said, "I'm sorry. I didn't mean to--"

Cash held up a hand to stop him. "It's fine. I couldn't hack it, and it's better that we found out before there was anything real on the line."

"They should have given you another chance," Patrick said.

"Yeah, but if they had I wouldn't have started my exciting career as a barista. No looking back, right?"

"Cash..."

"It's fine, Patrick. I'm at peace with what happened. And I'm glad I got as far in my training as I did, because that's how I found you, and you are worth all of it."

Patrick drug his thumb across Cash's lips, and Cash pulled him into a kiss, which Patrick returned.

When they had to come up for air, Cash said, "So, if you're done breaking our dishes, you should probably get going."

"Yeah," Patrick said. "My ride is two minutes out."

"Be careful, okay?" Cash said, kissing him again. He pulled away to add, "Don't get lost. Come back to me." He traced his fingers through Patrick's short black hair.

"Always..." Patrick said.

"Because if you don't, I'm coming after you. There's no power on Earth that could stop me."

Cash spent the next forty-eight hours in a crash course refresher on what, exactly, he was supposed to do. It had been three months, after all. He was a little surprised that Bakshi didn't just throw him into the deep end, since he was, after all, a wash-out. But it seemed like the agency wanted to give him a chance to actually be successful. Three other lives depended on it, as well as his own. Not to mention the fate of the world.

He watched and listened to the recordings of the three other runs. Brady had only been present in the slipstream for about thirty seconds before fading away and losing himself. Sasha made it an hour, and her time had ended with a stream of incessant babbling just before she'd faded. Patrick had made it the farthest, about three hours, but had not been able to penetrate a brane and had eventually come untethered from reality entirely. It seemed like they'd each tried to maintain their focus on their goal, and while that was usually a winning strategy, there was something about the slipstream that frustrated that. Maybe the key was not to have any certain idea in mind of what reality should look like, but be open to whatever the senses encountered.

The slipstream was outside of space and time. If he could find the others, they might still be alive. That was his hope.

Bakshi found him just after his final suit-fitting. "Remember your mission," she said. "If you find the others, it's a bonus. But we need you to break through, somewhere. Break through and set the anchor point so we can set up a permanent connection."

"I know my mission," Cash said. "But if I find them, I'm not going to leave them there."

"I'm not asking you to," Bakshi said. "Just...that's not your priority. If this is successful, we can make other runs, devoted to rescue."

"If I'm your last hope, then I'm going to do things my way."

Bakshi's lovely dark eyes narrowed, but her lips broke into a smile as she said, "Well, obviously, our way is not working."

"I need you to make me a promise," Cash said. "If I'm lost, you won't give up, you'll train others to find the lost ones. I don't care about myself, but Patrick, especially."

"I'll do what I can, but if this doesn't work, it might be the end of the road," Bakshi said. "Focus on your mission, and let me worry about the rest, okay?"

"I guess I can do that," Cash said. He was going to have to focus on one thing at a time, which was something he'd never been very good at. As he waited, he practiced his meditation exercises, trying to slow his rapidly beating heart.

As the time came closer when he would be running into the slipstream, Liesl worked on making sure all of his comms equipment was up and running.

"I'll be in your ear the entire time," she said, a smile on her plump face. Her hands were shaking as she adjusted the settings on the communications devices, and she pulled once or twice on her long blonde braid.

"Did you work with the others?" Cash asked her.

"I worked with Brady and Patrick," Liesl said, her voice sad. "I tried to keep them centered, but in the end they just...they just discohered and fell away."

"Do you think they're still alive?"

"I don't know what to think about that," Liesl said. "They had air for a while, but the slipstream is beyond time, so..."

"Time might not even be passing for them," Cash said. Liesl handed him back his helmet. He donned it, hearing a series of beeps in his ear. After a moment, the beeps were replaced by Liesl's voice. "Cash, can you hear me?"

He looked at her as he answered, her voice in his ear and also coming at him through the mask of his helmet. He nodded and gave her a thumbs-up sign. Liesl returned the thumbs-up, and then walked away, headed toward the control booth.

The control booth looked out over the main runway, but its windows were darkened, so Cash had no idea who, besides Liesl, was even in there. He supposed Bakshi, at least, would be watching and monitoring him. Maybe one or two of her bosses.

All around him the facility had the look of a place that was in the process of being dismantled. There'd once been workspace for dozens, with panels of instruments and walls full of screens. Most of that was gone now, leaving just the runway in place in the center of the cavernous space.

The technicians who would open the gate swarmed him as he moved into position, just in front of the spot where the gate would open.

"Ready, Bancroft?" Bakshi said in his ear.

A technician had just finishing installing his oxygen tank and filters, and he felt the difference when his suit switched over to the canned stuff. He felt light-headed for a moment as his brain got used to the increased oxygen content. There was a moment of euphoria. He was about to run outside the universe! He would find a new world to save the old, and he was going to be reunited with Patrick. At that moment, all of this seemed inevitable.

"Bancroft, I asked you a question," Bakshi said again.

"I think I have to go to the bathroom," Cash said, laughing.

"That's why you're wearing a diaper." She did not seem amused, but she never seemed amused about anything.

"I'm ready to go, Major Bakshi," he said calmly, and saluted the dark windows.

The lights dimmed as technicians fell into place around him. There was a long stretch of floor in front of him, lined with sensors and workstations. Six people would be monitoring the gate, making sure it stayed open, and reading everything his suit sent back about the slipstream as he ran through it.

"Cash, you're sure about this?" It was Liesl, her voice quiet in his ear. She was risking her career by even asking him that question, but it said a lot about the kind of person she was that she wanted him to be sure. He knew she would shut down the entire operation if Cash so much as flinched.

So he didn't. Even as his heart raced, he said calmly, "I've been ready for this for a long time."

The lights around him flashed, then everything went dark. He could hear nothing from outside his suit. He didn't even hear Liesl breathing, which meant she must have turned her microphone off.

Then Liesl counted down from ten. At three, lightning arced from two sources on either side of the pathway. The lightning formed into a circle, then a sphere, and then the sphere opened.

There was no way Cash could describe what he saw when he looked at that opening. It was a smear of colors, flashing from one to the other.

Cash ran forward and launched himself into the gate.

In training, they'd stepped into the slipstream for mere seconds at a time to ensure they could withstand it. A few looked at that non-space, and their brains broke. They couldn't handle what they saw, and had to be pulled back, sobbing. Of their original cohort of seven, only three had completed their training.

Cash had never had that problem. The Slipstream was...to say it was beautiful would be saying it had physical attributes, and that was not true at all. The Slipstream was a non-place. The place between places. And it looked like everything and nothing. He couldn't perceive it. He couldn't stop perceiving it.

There was nothing stable to look at and at the same time too much to focus on. Images coalesced in front of him, images that, it had been explained to him, were only his brain's pitiful human way of making sense of what it saw. But there was no sense to be made. There was nothing here in the space between.

His feet left the floor and sailed into the slipstream, and there was nothing beneath him anymore, nothing holding him up, nothing to push against. Yet he made the same motions he had when running, and he felt like he was moving—a physical sensation, since the space around him was made of nothing, so there were no landmarks to mark his progress. But he risked a glance behind him, finding the gate a pinprick of light. He had no idea how far away from it he was because far away was a concept that no longer mattered.

He opened himself up to the slipstream. Liesl's voice crackled in his head. "You still okay?" she asked him.

"I'm great. This is great. What could possibly be wrong?" Cash said back, but in truth, he couldn't focus on Liesl, who was his last tether to the real world. No, he needed to sail into the nothing, into the non-space, and see what he could find there.

Here was where they'd been trained to focus, to concentrate on any tendril of nothing that might lead them to something, whatever that meant. And that was why Cash had failed out. He'd been unable to maintain his focus long enough to bring an image into reality. But he had a feeling now that was the wrong approach anyway. He opened his eyes to everything he saw, everything his senses told him, anchoring himself on the sensation of air being pumped over his face.

Liesl was saying something, but her voice faded in and out. Cash found himself not minding that. He thought she was asking him to report what he was seeing, but how could he do that? He had no concept for anything that his eyes took in. His brain, though, his brain felt like it had an itch that was finally being scratched. Open to the everything that was around him, he felt like he was taking it all in. Every non-sensation, every non-feeling. Is this what the others had felt? Was this what Patrick had felt?

If he wanted to, he could be lost here, become part of this nothing-that-was-everything and just exist, beyond time and space. Part of him desperately yearned for that. The Slipstream seemed like the place he'd been destined to find, like finally he had the key to unlock the universe.

And then he heard it. Was Liesl humming?

"What is that song?" he asked her. It was lovely, and he didn't recognize it.

"What song, Cash?" Liesl asked him, her voice calm.

"You were humming."

"I wasn't. My microphone was off."

"Huh." Cash listened more intently. It sounded like singing, but it was unlike any voice he'd ever heard before. Opening himself up to all of it at once, he heard it louder in his ears. It didn't sound like it was coming from his coms. "Do you hear that music?"

"You're hearing music?" Liesl said.

"Like singing. Distant."

"How many voices?"

"I don't know. It's kind of hard to describe."

When he tried to concentrate on the sound, it faded, so he did what he did best, listened without focusing on it, letting his consciousness dance ever so lightly over the sound without attaching to it. And when he did, it got louder. When he pivoted a certain way, aimed in a certain direction, it grew more discordant, voices out of tune with themselves and with the universe. But in other directions, it grew sweeter, more in tune. He followed the lovelier sounds, hoping they could be a reliable guide. But he had to do it almost without meaning to, without letting the voices know that he was listening.

He had the impression that the voices weren't human, or were somehow beyond human. Or maybe it was every human, or every being in the universe, reaching out to him, calling him. Every being in our universe, or possibly in another.

"Did anyone else report hearing music?" Cash asked Liesl.

"Patrick asked me if I was humming, like you did, but neither Sasha or Brady said anything about it."

He had to release his attention from Liesl's voice now because he had a thought about what the music meant. Maybe the song was guiding him into a habitable space? He didn't know how he knew that, but he had a sense that he was right, somehow.

Could the music lead him to Patrick?

He turned his head in every direction, letting the song wash over his ears and give him a direction to try and run through, if what he was doing could even still be called running. Certain patterns emerged in the light around him now, and they seemed coordinated with the music. How could nothingness coordinate with anything? It was a question he asked himself, but it felt dangerous to consider too closely, as if he thought too hard about it, this little bubble of non-reality would pop and he would be left in interstellar space, or some other worse place.

Maybe the music was something his brain was doing to him? If so, maybe his brain was finding a pathway through the nothing that would lead to something. That was his goal, right?

Soon he felt himself drifting closer, the music growing louder. And then from out of the nothing came something—a body, seemingly wrapped in the music, its arms flailing at either side. Cash grabbed hold of the body as he continued to propel himself, pulled along by the music. The body wore the same kind of suit he was wearing, its blocky oxygen tank pressing into Cash's chest. He couldn't maneuver it well enough to turn it so he could see its face. He just had to hope it was who he wanted it to be.

The singing grew more intense. There were words now, but they were words in a language he'd never spoken and would never be able to speak. He sensed no hostile intent, and he leaned into the melody, turning away from discordance.

Once more, if he tried to focus on it, it would fade, so he kept his mind open to everything. He had no idea how much time had passed. It felt at once like it had been ten seconds or ten years since he'd leapt into the slipstream. His mind had been made to listen to this music, to be guided by it. For everything his bastard brain had cost him over the years, he supposed he should have been grateful.

He had no idea if the body in his arms was alive or dead. He could barely hold onto it as the music rose around him, growing louder and more intense. It was so loud now that he couldn't even hear Liesl, who must surely be saying something.

And then all the colors he had never known existed flowed around him, and he felt himself breaking through something. It was all he could do to hold onto the body he carried, as reality coalesced around him once more and he fell into a kaleidoscope of purple shades.

Cash had no idea how long he'd been out when he last came back to consciousness. It was Liesl's voice in his ear that brought him back.

"Cash, come in. We can still hear you breathing. Cash, come in."

"Hey," Cash said, before he opened his eyes. The ground beneath him was soft as far as he could tell. Something had cushioned his fall. "I'm alive."

"Oh, thank God," Liesl said. "We thought we'd lost you too."

Cash opened his eyes. He was lying on his side. Pain spasmed from his nearly-dislocated shoulder. On the bottom half of his vision was a field of pale white sand and on the top was a stretch of purple that looked like the sky, but everyone knew the sky wasn't purple. To his left was a line of trees with bushy yellow leaves, and to his right was an expanse of turquoise sea.

"Can you tell me where I am?" Cash said, pushing himself up into a sitting position. His body hurt all over. However he'd gotten here, he must have landed hard.

"We'll know more once you set the anchor and attach the beacon," Liesl said. "Tell me what you see."

Cash did. After a moment, she said, her voice low, "Cash. I think you did it."

"Unless I'm on earth and my vision is just really messed up after being in the slipstream."

"I don't think that's it."

He brought up his system interface and found that the air was a slightly different combination of elements from the air on earth, but it was breathable. Before he could think better of it, he unlatched his helmet, breathing in the air. It smelled slightly sweet and felt humid in his nostrils.

Then he saw the body sprawled on the sand about a dozen paces away. Cash cursed and crawled across the sand to the body's side.

The body's faceplate was spider-webbed, and Cash still had no idea who it was. He unlatched the helmet and pulled it off.

Patrick. His forehead bled, his eyes closed. But it was Patrick. Cash almost sobbed at that moment, but he had to see if Patrick was still alive. Was he even breathing?

He reported his find to Liesl. "Thank God," she responded.

Cash placed his hand against Patrick's chest, feeling it rise and fall. Then Patrick lurched back to life, turning on his side. He coughed, trying to push himself up, then fell back down. Cash caught him.

"Cash?" Patrick said, incredulous. He blinked several times, as if trying to make sure that what he was seeing was real.

"It's me," Cash said, then he embraced Patrick, ignoring the pain in his own shoulder.

"What's happening?" Patrick asked.

"You got lost," Cash said.

Patrick wiped the white sand out of his eyes and said, "I guess I did. And you found me."

"I told you I would," Cash said, and then he kissed Patrick. Patrick's mouth was warm and wet against his, and he pushed his face against Cash's, raising his arms to hold him in place.

Afterward, they set the anchor point and the beacon, so others could follow them through. Then they waited so Patrick's helmet could be replaced. Cash didn't care how long it took, he was never letting go of Patrick again.

He had no idea what kind of world he had found, if it would be suitable to save humanity. But now he knew how to get through the slipstream. He would help the agency find others like him, people who could hear the music that waited for them between worlds.

He still heard the slipstream's song, and hoped it was just a memory. He rested his head on Patrick's shoulder, and closed his eyes.

Chad Grayson has worked as a phone service rep for various tech companies, a gas station attendant, a middle school language arts and history teacher, and even spent one night cutting the mold off the cheese at the cheese factory. He spends most of his time writing, reading, hiking, gaming, painting miniatures, and binge-watching Netflix. His superpowers, besides ADHD, are procrastination and dyscalculia. He lives near his children in Cottonwood, California, with his fiancé, Jimmy, and an assortment of pets, including a very bossy cat. He is an associate member of SFWA. You can find him online at chadgrayson.com (where you can sign up for his monthly newsletter featuring exclusive posts, previews, book reviews, and updates) and on mastodon as @ChadGrayson@mastodon.other-worldsink.com, and on Threads as c.e.grayson. Follow him on Facebook at facebook.com/ChadGraysonAuthor.

THE SECRETS OF DARKHORN

B.A. BOOHER

Toklo tied his tribe's blue-and-orange tassel to the last stone on his wife's cairn. The stones stood over her grave on the river island in the middle of the frozen basin. The frost in his beard helped him maintain his stoic demeanor in front of his father, the tribe's chieftain. The old warrior pressed in close against his son. "You honor her well."

"The wyrdresses say she was strong in her battle to bear my son," Toklo said.

His father wrapped his arm around Toklo's shoulder. "The ferrous giants don't normally cross the ice. You were where a hunter should have been."

"And now my wife is on the final hunt." Toklo wiped his eyes. He smelled smoke. A black cloud rose from the northern edge of the island. "I would see my son now."

Toklo's father pulled him along to the south. "It is fine that you remember Yura, but do not mistake muddled waters for a true reflection. She gave us her sorrow."

Toklo jerked his arm away. "What've you done?"

The chieftain rushed to get between Toklo and the smoke. "To end its suffering is just. Leave it and let your next wife bring you a son."

A baby's cry echoed in the river basin.

"I will not abandon him," Toklo said.

"You want the sorrow? Take nothing but the ax on your belt. None of the tribe's provisions, not one of our spears or bows. No tent, sled, or powderwolf."

"Small price for a son," Toklo said.

Twenty yards off the northern coast, black smoke billowed from a ring, a marker of the offering. The idea was to let the newborn die from the cold, so it never had to feel an animal's teeth. Sorrows, those newborns malformed or too weak to thrive, were offered to the gods to keep the tribe strong.

Toklo hopped the smoldering ring, but where he expected to see his son was only a clear patch where the child had melted the snow. The only tracks were from the clan's sleds and mukluks. No frost jackals or blue gilas had braved the black smoke to feast on the malformed babe, so where was he?

An owl swooped down for a winter hare on the western bank. A trail of footprints dropped from the embankment and crossed those from the tribe. A second pair returned the same way and climbed the snowy shore.

Toklo charged into the woods, jogging through the ankle-high snow. Whenever he crossed a frozen stream, the Darkhorn mountain loomed in the distance. His father said the Darkhorn was full of witchy, baneful things. Toklo wanted to rescue his son before the spire's shadow fell on the child.

The day marched on to the rhythm of Toklo's breathing and the crunch of snow under his mukluks. When the snow fell so heavy it seemed to drag the sun down, he worried the trail would be covered. For the gods, the baby cried, his wail echoing through the wooded valley. How could the midwives have ever thought the child with those lungs a sorrow?

"Yes, little one!" Toklo said after a thunderous outburst. He swore he could hear Yura's obstinance in the child's scream. Defying the taboo of naming a sorrow, Toklo decided to call the child Silyur, the breath of Yura.

Night unfurled, a campfire flickered on the horizon, and the husky snicker of frost jackals answered the child's cries. Toklo counted three sets of blinking, white eyes heading toward the camp and charged ahead. Silyur's cries admonished him for his slowness. The jackals circled the campfire. Toklo shouted a warning, and they snickered. They leaped into the small clearing where the campfire burned. A man's shout punctuated Silyur's cries. Toklo snatched his ax from his belt and sprinted. Snarls entwined with the swish and flutter of a swinging torch. Feral shadows darted between the trees and across Toklo, staccato beats of vision against the campfire's glare. On the far side of the fire, a diminutive man with his back against a tamarack stood above a wicker basket heaped with blankets. He held a shepherd's crook tucked tight behind his right arm so the hook was above his head. A faint glow glimmered along the hook. He chanted a strange, desperate incantation. "Gyato! Nyima! Sempha!"

The incantation had no effect. The size of small ponies, the frost jackals circled the camp, eying the man. Snow clung to the barbed quills of their manes. Jagged ice dangled and clinked on their chins. Each time they approached, the man swung his crook and fended them off.

One of the jackals leapt forward and snapped its jaws. The man spun the crook, but the jackal pranced back and dodged the swing. It was a feint as another jackal lunged at the man's exposed side. The man quickly swung the staff around to strike the beast's snout. The crook sparked, and the smell of singed fur wafted in the air.

Leaping into the clearing, Toklo barreled into the jackal's flank. Beast and man rolled in the snow until Toklo kicked the animal off. It landed in a cloud of snow and spun around to see Toklo regain his feet. While it paced looking for the best angle of attack, Toklo shuffled over so that the tree was at his back and the man by his side.

"Thank you," the man said. Judging by the long, angular nose jutting over the man's white scarf, Toklo took the man for an Arunian. But that didn't make sense. No Arun village stood within raiding distance since Toklo was a boy.

"I'm here for my son," Toklo said.

"Your son?" the man asked, but one of the jackals leaped, its jaw snapping in the air. Toklo spun, swinging the ax into the jackal's ribs and throwing it against the tree. The wounded jackal scurried into the trees to lick its wound and snarl.

The Arunian chanted again. "Whatever gods you're praying to, they're not answering," Toklo said. "So cease your blather lest you attract worse."

The jackals circled, unsure about the newest enemy. Two of them stood between Toklo and the injured third. They alternated between snarls and sneers as they paced back and forth. Toklo squared his stance and prepared for an attack, but the jackals snapped their jaws shut. Their ears perked, the ground trembled, and large clumps of snow fell from the branches.

With a huff, the jackals fled.

"What spooked them?" Toklo asked. A black spear flew through the trees. The spear elicited a sharp whimper from the jackal before the beast fell limp, pinned to a white ash tree.

Branches cracked and broke as a ferrous giant charged through the wood. Moonlight glistened off his metal skullcap and down his arm. With a hand as large as Toklo's chest, the giant swatted the hunter aside. Toklo smacked into a trunk and toppled through the branches to the frozen ground. The giant continued on, out of sight.

The Arunian hunkered down and used his glowing hook to get a better look. "You Iakashi certainly are made of strong stuff," he said.

"My son," whispered Toklo. "Where is my son?"

The man stared. His head twitched and dipped down until his shoulders curled and his whole torso writhed. Then, like a released spring, he sighed. "Took him from the ring of fire. The child's a sorrow."

Through gritted teeth, Toklo said, "Stolen from me."

The man chewed his lip. "Kid's a sorrow, Iakashi. He belongs to the Rivet Witch now. The sooner you accept that, the better."

"No."

The Arunian's face pinched before relaxing. "I was afraid you were going to say that," he said. He pressed the glowing hook into Toklo's chest. Pain erupted through his body as Toklo's muscles seized. Luckily, his body had already endured enough trauma, and the agony dissolved in darkness.

An osprey's cry woke Toklo. He sat up, pine needles clinging to his limbs. He felt the singed circle where the shepherd's crook had stung him. Toklo had never seen such magic. The Arunian had left Toklo's ax lodged in the trunk above a crudely carved message, Go Home.

Toklo jerked the ax from the trunk and winced. His side hurt with every breath, but nothing seemed broken. Carefully, he crawled out from under the branches. The snow had slackened to a light dusting. The coals from the campfire still smoldered. The giant had tamped down the area, but there were still holes in the snow made by the man's crook. Eventually, the crook's divots disappeared, but the giant's tracks were easy to follow. Even as the snow kept falling, it would take hours for the trail to fill in, and the broken and bent branches still marked the giant's passing.

Toklo followed the giant's tracks into the woods. As the Darkhorn loomed, the trees grew twisted and gnarled. Black vines clung to the trees, and thorny bushes dominated the forest floor under the snow. Large outcroppings of rocks jutted out between the vegetation. Immense cairns of stacked stones dotted the landscape. Some were simple piles, while others were stacked in the shape of people. Were these some kind of mockery of the Iakashi cairns?

Near the end of the second day, a set of footprints appeared beside the giant's. The initial set was side-by-side and deep as if the Arunian had jumped from the giant's shoulders. His footprints diverged from the giant's trajectory toward the Darkhorn. If Toklo chose the wrong trail, he might lose his son forever. Ultimately, Toklo decided the Arunian would be easier to question if the child was not with him.

The path wound through several cairns. The footprints stopped and faced each of them, sometimes circling the rocks to always get to the side that faced the Darkhorn. Were the cairns monuments to the mountain? Toklo could not discern any difference between the Darkhorn-facing sides and those facing away. He did not think that the cairns were Arunian in nature. As a boy, one of Toklo's first raids had been on an Arun settlement, and he didn't remember seeing any cairns there. The Arunians burned their dead and worshiped some kind of water god. The few Arun missionaries who had come to Toklo's tribe had taken a dim view of the Iakashi wyrdresses, calling them witches and trying to convert them away from their gods. No cairns marked the missionaries' graves.

Just as night's shroud obscured the trail, Toklo spotted an orange glow in the distance. Ax in hand, he crept toward the light, careful to stay close to bush or tree. In a small clearing ringed with bushes between three redwoods, the Arunian sat facing away from Toklo and into the fire. His white scarf fluttered from beneath the broad-rimmed hat.

Toklo scanned the area for signs there might be giants nearby, but the Arunian appeared alone. A hare roasted over the crackling fire. Toklo suppressed the anxiety welling within his chest. The child could be asleep or even just quiet.

The bushes had a small break directly behind where the Arunian sat. Toklo silently gave thanks and pulled a knife from his belt. He could have thrown his ax or blade into the Arunian's back, but Toklo couldn't talk to a dead man if Silyur wasn't there. With knife in hand, Toklo pushed through the snow rather than let it crunch beneath his feet. The Arunian gave no sign of noticing Toklo's approach.

From the bushes, Toklo pounced, leaping across the snow to tackle the Arunian. His arms wrapped around the man's shoulders only for them to collapse in Toklo's grasp. Something wrapped around his ankles and hefted him upward so that he hung, upside-down, in a cloud of upended snow that sizzled in the campfire.

"I thought you were never going to go for the bait," the Arunian said. "Thought I was going to be in that tree all night."

Toklo twisted in the snare, trying to see where the voice was coming from but only saw the Arunian's empty hat and cloak on the snow. He grabbed his ax and tried to swing it at the vine holding him. The attempt brought a blinding stab of pain along his side, but he also saw the Arunian hiding in a tree.

"That looked like it hurt," the Arunian said. He slid down from the tree and gathered his hat and cloak. A metal plate glinted at the base of his skull.

Seeing Toklo's ineffectual swiping, the Arunian hooked Toklo's wrist with his crook and twisted until Toklo dropped his ax. "Now we can be civilized," the Arunian said. His face contorted as if he had tasted something bitter. When he relaxed, he wrapped his scarf around his mouth and chin, pulled on his cloak, and donned his hat before vigorously brushing off his thighs. "So, to whom am I speaking?"

Toklo swung on the vine, trying to reach for the snare. He gave up and he fell back into a cloud of his exhalations. "I am Toklo, son of…I am Toklo."

The Arunian chuckled. "I am Elkin, also son of. Did I not get the runes right in my message? That's it, isn't it? I didn't get the runes right." Again, he swiped his hands repeatedly against his thighs.

"I'll go home when I get my son."

"Oh, so I did get it right." Elkin smiled. "Iakashi runes always look so simple but are deceptively nuanced, no?"

Swinging over the fire left Toklo feeling hot and impatient. "Where is my son?"

Elkin rubbed his thighs again before answering, "Look, I'm trying to help you. You saw the sorrow. You know it will never join the hunt you Iakashi value so much."

"I never saw my child. He was taken while I dealt with my wife's death. And if he can't run the hunt, what does the Rivet Witch want with him?" Toklo braced himself for the coming agony before reaching for his ankles.

From his cloak, Elkin fished out a hunk of wood and whittled as he talked. "Well, she won't leave him to die like your people did."

"I left them, didn't I?" Toklo reached for the snare again but caught it this time. The knot was tight at his ankles. His sides ached like he was being crushed, but he held on anyway.

Elkin's shoulders twisted, then his arms. When he relaxed, he sucked in the cold air and let it out slowly. "She can help him run and grow and have a life. Would you deny him that?"

Toklo grimaced as he forced his thumbs into the snare's knot. "Of course not, but why must she keep my son to heal him?"

"I suppose she would have to answer that. If you're really so determined, I can take you to her."

"I'll go with you, then." Toklo's thumbs had managed to wiggle enough room in the knot for him to start unraveling the vine. He made slow progress until he suddenly dropped into the snow.

Elkin tucked his knife away. Beside him, the severed vine swung. He handed Toklo his ax and said, "We've got some walking to do if we're to be there by morning."

A frozen river cut through the hillside bank a few miles north of the camp. They walked single file on the ice, Elkin at the lead, until they reached a long, frozen lake. The ice groaned and cracked under their weight, muffled by a blanket of snow glittering in dawn's pink rays. A soft wind sifted snow across the lake in ephemeral tendrils that coalesced into shifting drifts. Rocky hills curved along the lake's shoreline like giant ripples frozen in time after the Darkhorn had been driven into the northern end. A silver waterfall cascaded to the lake and churned water in defiance of the cold.

Throughout the journey, Elkin shivered, not continuously or with a brush of a cold wind, but randomly. Toklo eventually asked if the Arunian wanted his cloak.

"What? Why?" Elkin asked.

"You keep shivering."

"Oh, that," Elkin said. "Thank you for the offer, but my cloak is plenty warm. The twitching is just something I do."

"You palsied?"

Elkin grunted and shook his head. "Something like that."

The roar of falling water filled the air but was quickly muted by the dark spruce forest that lined the shores. The trees leaned in toward one another in a creaking conspiracy of judgment for the men who approached the bleak walls of the Darkhorn.

Two ferrous giants huddled around a firepit outside a massive gate carved into the mountain's base. Laughter, like gargling tar, littered their snarling growls. One had an iron jaw that creaked when he spoke, while the other had metal legs shaped like a wolf's.

"Elkin," snarled one of the giants, "who you bring?"

"Yeah, who you bring, Elkin?"

Elkin waved his hands disarmingly. "This gentleman is the new sorrow's father."

The giants' eyes widened. Iron-Jaw bent down and poked Toklo with a finger the size of the Iakashi's lower leg. "Father?"

Toklo's hand fell to his ax, but Elkin pushed Iron-Jaw's finger away. "He needs to speak with Mother," Elkin said.

The giants looked at one another before Steel-Leg said, "No visitors."

"Send for her." Elkin's face pinched before he added, "If we're outside, we're passersby. She doesn't have rules about passersby."

The giants looked from Elkin to each other, to Toklo, to the gate, and then back to Elkin. When they started another circuit, Elkin took his crook from his belt and said, "Go!"

The giants huffed but opened the gate just wide enough to pass before pulling it closed behind them. Toklo watched them go and then asked, "You're the witch's son?"

"She took me in when I was six." Elkin brushed his thighs before putting the crook back in his belt. "When my blood mother was certain she couldn't cleanse me of whatever made me tic, my father took me into the woods and strapped me to a tree. Said if the great god wanted me to wiggle and squirm, I'd wiggle and squirm right out of my bindings. Nearly froze to death before the Rivet Witch found me. I was too old for most of her treatments, but I could learn."

"Is that why you bring her sorrows?"

"I suppose." Elkin's face twisted before cracking into a smile. "I always wondered if my father ever returned and saw the empty bindings. I can only imagine what he would have thought."

Toklo fell silent as he thought about what he would say to the Rivet Witch. Or at least, he tried to, but his mind kept returning to the idea that Elkin had held his son. Toklo could not restrain himself any longer. "What does my son look like?"

"Huh? Oh, you know, little," Elkin said.

"Do you think that's why the wyrdresses said he was a sorrow?"

Elkin shook his head until his shoulders curled in. When the tic passed, he said, "There was a..." but fell silent as the gate swung open.

Compared to the giants, the Rivet Witch was short, standing only as tall as Toklo. She wore a hat similar to Elkin's but with a lace veil. Elkin opened his arms to greet her, but she raised her hand to stop him. Steel claws capped her fingertips while small wires ran to gears aside each of her knuckles. "Why have you brought this Iakashi to my door?"

"Please, you have..." Toklo said, but the witch silenced him with a finger.

"He claims his son is the sorrow Sempha brought," Elkin said.

"Did the black billows blow?" the witch asked. Elkin nodded. "Then the sorrow was already given."

"He was set out while I buried his mother. I would never abandon my son," Toklo protested.

"That is of no concern to me," the Rivet Witch said. She eyed Elkin rubbing his thighs. "Is that a new tic? It's been a while since you had a treatment."

"I'm fine, Mother." Elkin relayed the story of the jackals. "If Toklo had not rushed in, I'm not sure I would have survived long enough for Sempha to save me. Even after being injured, he kept coming. I've never seen a father work so hard to get his sorrow back."

The Rivet Witch turned to study Toklo. She came so close he could feel the veil flutter with her breath. When she suddenly withdrew, Toklo could not help but let his hand go for his ax.

"You want the sorrow back?" the witch asked.

Toklo released his grip and let the ax hang in its belt loop. "His name is Silyur, and yes."

The witch ran a finger along her chin. "You can have the child."

Toklo sucked in a blast of cold air. "Thank you!"

"I'm sorry you had to go through all of this," the witch said. "Now, this time of year, the eastern shore has the best selection of rocks, certainly better than anything you'll find on your way back to your tribe."

"Rocks?" Toklo asked.

The witch waved her hand toward the eastern shoreline. "River rocks mainly, but there are some quartz and obsidian pieces, too. You'll be able to make the wee one a splendid cairn."

Toklo sprang forward, ax in hand. "What did you—"

The witch's hand caught him by the throat, cutting off his air and lifting him up. "What have I done?" the witch asked. "Not enough. Without my help, the sorrow will die before the sun rises again. If you wish to take your son, you want him to die."

Elkin stepped closer to the witch. "Mother, he could be of use. I'm no tracker. Toklo is. Nyima is still missing. We could use Toklo to find her."

The Rivet Witch eyed Toklo. "He doesn't want my help."

Toklo squirmed in her grip and fought to speak. "No, I...do want... it. Please...will do...any...thing."

The witch dropped Toklo into the snow. He gasped for air as she spoke. "If you bring back my child, we can discuss yours. But if you return without Nyima, only death will await you here. Understand?"

Gray twilight threatened a winter's storm over the gulch. A biting wind whipped up snow as shadows took on a blue hue. Toklo led Elkin down the path to the bottom of the ravine. A snowshoe crane lifted from its perch and glided down the gorge. A blue gila squawked, and the white field mice and winter hares sprinted for cover.

Toklo crouched by a small patch of golden snow. He swiped two fingers through the amber frost and rubbed them against his thumb before sniffing the oily residue. "She paused here. Fluid's runnier. We're close."

He did not understand what the liquid was, but he did not need to. Elkin had tried to explain that it was something to do with making the giant's limbs move, but it wasn't blood. Whatever the fluid, the golden droplets left an easy, reliable trail to a cave at the end of the gulch.

At the mouth of the cave, Elkin held his crook aloft, and it glowed white. "Nyima? Are you in there?"

A hoarse rumble bellowed out of the dark, "Elkin?" Heavy footfalls stumbled inside the cave. The giantess emerged. She had one immense good leg but had to drag the other through the cave.

"Nyima, what happened?" Elkin asked.

Her face darkened as she slowly enunciated each syllable. "Got lost."

Elkin looked her over. "Why are you dragging your foot? Let me look you over."

Nyima had to use her hands to manipulate her metal leg so she could sit. Even then, she towered over Toklo and Elkin. Two spears had lodged into her back beneath a metal hump that rose to her shoulders. He jerked one out but left the other alone. "It's punctured one of the hydraulic lines. If I remove it, I'm scared she'll lose all her fluid. How'd you manage this, Nyima?"

The giantess searched the clouds for her answer. Her mouth fell slack as a glob of drool dribbled over her lip. Her pink tongue occasionally poked up from her immense underbite as she spoke. "I was hungry. Followed my nose to the shore. There were little ones on the ice. Cooking. On the ice! I warn them. Not safe on ice. Maybe if I warn them, they share. But they got mad."

Nyima seemed to see Toklo for the first time. Her face darkened, and she roared. "Little ones is mean. Scream and cut me." She pushed onto her fists, but Elkin stepped between her and Toklo.

"Nyima, you don't hate me, do you? You love Elkin, right?" She huffed but reluctantly nodded. However, as soon as she saw Toklo again, she growled and pounded on the ground. Elkin waved his crook to get the giantess's attention while waving Toklo away. He slipped behind Nyima while Elkin soothed her.

While Nyima mulled over Elkin's words, Toklo saw a blue-and-orange tassel fluttering atop a mound of snow. He grabbed the tassel and pulled on it, freeing the spear Elkin had pulled from Nyima's back.

An Iakashi spear. All the events from the giantess's story fell into place. He saw it all happening and stumbled back.

"Toklo?" Elkin said.

Toklo held the broken spear like an offering. "Do you know what this is? Do you see this tassel? It's the colors of my tribe. My wife could have thrown this defending our camp. This is why she went into labor early."

Elkin put himself between Nyima and Toklo. "Toklo, put the ax away."

Toklo held the spear in one hand and his ax in the other. His hands shook with rage as he glared at Nyima. "She killed my wife."

"Not on purpose," Elkin said. "You know that. It was a misunderstanding. Your people got scared, spooked Nyima, and your wife went into labor. Nyima, tell him you're sorry."

Nyima looked at Toklo. Tears welled along her saucer eyes. "I sorry," she grumbled.

"Your wife is gone, Toklo, but you can still have your son."

Toklo raised his weapons and, with a cry of rage, threw them to the ground. His chest heaved, and his jaw trembled. "I want my son."

As they neared the gulch's opening, a powderwolf howled and was answered by a tundra goose's yawp. Toklo stiffened at the sounds.

"What is it?" Elkin asked, but Toklo shushed him.

When the goose answered the howl again, Toklo said, "They're triangulating. It's an Iakashi hunting party. They said they were going to hunt her down."

Elkin grimaced. "What do you suggest? Hide in the cave?"

Toklo looked at the dribble of golden fluid trailing behind them. "There's no way they won't find her there."

"Can you explain what happened?" Elkin asked.

Toklo shook his head. "No, and they won't care about my son."

"We can't fight them," Elkin said.

Toklo put his hands on his hips and eyed the gulch, looking for a way out. "We'll have to give them what they want."

Atop the edge of the gulch, Toklo sat in a pool of amber liquid and warmed himself by the campfire. He was careful not to get too close as Elkin had warned him the fluid could be flammable.

He did not need to wait long before several of his old tribe emerged from the darkness. They looked at him from a distance, too scared to come close to the golden man. Eventually, one Iakashi stepped forward, spear raised, and asked, "Toklo, son of Beshoar, is that you?"

"I am Toklo," he said.

The chieftain came forward. "Toklo, what are you doing out here? What are you covered in?"

"The ferrous giant's blood. I lured him into the ravine and then dropped a rock on him. You can see his leg if you look," Toklo said. The broken spear lay at his feet. He offered it to the chieftain. "Yura has been avenged."

"It is a mighty warrior who can slay the ferrous giant. You have honored your tribe, your father, and your wife," the chieftain said. "We will sing songs of this day. Come, we shall have a feast in your honor."

"Go ahead. I am must cleanse myself first. I will return in three days."

At the Darkhorn, the three were quickly admitted through the gate. Nyima was helped to the infirmary while Sempha led Elkin and Toklo through immense tunnels lined with orbs of light set into the walls. The giant took them to a large cavern filled with gigantic glass tanks. The Rivet Witch met them in front of one of the tanks nestled in a metal cradle. Toklo's son floated in one lit with a soft internal light.

"I suppose a broken leg can be overlooked," the Rivet Witch said. "Have your son, but without my continued care, he will not last long."

"I thought you'd heal him if I brought Nyima home," Toklo said.

"It's the vats that make them so big," the Rivet Witch said, "and makes them my children. What the vats don't correct, I supplement with iron and steel. If you want your son to survive, you need to let him stay here."

Elkin clasped Toklo's shoulder. "He'll be alive. Strong. Able to run. Isn't that what you want?"

What Toklo wanted was his son, not a giant with metal limbs. Was it better than burying him?

"If he is to stay here, I have one request."

Toklo cradled the child, shielding it from the wind ripping across the frozen river. The child's cry echoed along the banks sending sparrows into the air.

Elkin twitched beside them. "He's got a set of lungs on him."

"Indeed, brother," Toklo said, and he followed Elkin off the ice. Behind them, the smoke of sorrow billowed.

Bret Booher lives in Indiana with his wife, two sons, and their menagerie of pets. An English teacher passionate about writing and family, Bret found it perfectly natural to craft a story about a father refusing to give up on his son. Bret has constantly drawn strength and hope from his family when dealing with depression, and creating a character with Tourette's was a way to honor his son's constant struggle as well. Along with writing short stories, Bret co-hosts a YouTube channel called the Gored Ox Pub.

ESCAPE CHOICE

EMMA BURNETT

Dear Dr Baek,

We regret to inform you that there has been an incident with Max at school today during our mandatory evacuation drill.

Max will be required to stay after school tomorrow to repeat the drill, and we feel we need to meet with you to ensure this behaviour is taken seriously for everyone's safety.

Yours in voyage,
Maresa Lehrer

~

Max glanced at his mother's face. She had that line between her eyebrows, which sometimes meant that she was thinking, and sometimes meant she was annoyed. He looked briefly at his teacher, sitting across from them. Her face was too blank for him to interpret.

He looked out the window and started counting stars that looked blue.

"Max, it would help if you engaged in the conversation." His teacher had asked something, and wanted an answer.

He muttered, "I hate the escape pods."

"Yes, you've said that," his teacher said.

"I don't like getting into them. They have no alone space and they're too noisy. People touch me." He glanced at his mother. She nodded with what he thought might be encouragement. "They have no bathrooms."

"There's a flip out toilet in each one."

"It's not private." He looked back out the window. "I don't like them, is all."

"But...that doesn't matter. You're not supposed to like them. If there's an emergency, no one's particularly going to like them, are they?"

"All the other kids like the drills, though. I don't."

His teacher took a breath to reply, but his mother cut across her. "I really don't think this is helping," she said. "We've been trying to work through this for years. He's always had a problem with chaotic spaces."

Max hated when people talked about him while he was in the room, but they did it a lot. He crossed his legs on the chair and fidgeted with his fingernails, picking harder when their voices started to rise.

"I'm sorry, but I don't think you're dealing with this the right way," his mother snapped.

Maresa's face wasn't blank anymore, and her voice was edging towards the volume she used in a busy class. "Yeah, well, maybe I'm not cut out for this!"

"Maresa, you signed up for the job."

"I signed up to help teach half a dozen kids, ten years ago. No one predicted this bumper crop of kids." She looked down at her desk for a moment. "I didn't realise what I was signing on to."

"There's another option."

"Oh, come on. You know I'm a bad candidate for cryosleep. We both are. All those complications with people under thirty, and now," she gestured at Max. "It's not like we can go to sleep and leave them. I get that I'm not the ship's best teacher. I'm a road planner. I'll be properly useful when we arrive. But I'm trying, here."

Max was getting restless. The office was too bright, the chair's fabric too creaky. The adults were too loud, and anyway, he didn't like listening to them argue. He wanted to be in his quiet, tidy room.

Something moved across the window, blocking his view of the stars. He stared for a moment, then uncrossed his legs and walked to the window. He suddenly wished he could be the person blocking his view, and he touched his forehead to the glass.

"I want to do that," he said loudly. He pointed at the window, at the person doing a hull inspection. His mother and teacher looked at him, confused. "I want to be out there, where it's quiet. If I take care of our home, I'll never have to get in an emergency escape pod."

"But," his mother said, "But, Max, I'm a scientist."

"So?" His forehead scrunched.

"So, I...I just assumed you'd, you know, work with plants. Like me."

Max felt his stomach tighten. His mother worked in a busy laboratory. There were sharp smells and bright lights in there, and lots of people with elbows that bumped you. "Do I have to do what you do?"

"I never thought about it. I guess, maybe not?"

Maresa stared at Max for a moment, face unreadable again. Then she nodded. "Hmm. That's an idea, Max. I will talk to maintenance, find out what training you need to do in order to work with them." She smiled. "We need ship caretakers. It's a long journey."

～

Dear Max and Dr Baek,

. . .

Keeping you both in the loop. As you know, Max's training finished last week, but we can't offer him a position until he's prepared to do regular spacewalks. We'd like him to join the team, but he'll have to suit up and go out.

Max, we'd be excited to have you on the team. Please let me know your decision.

Best,

Wayan

~

Max was relieved to be done with a busy day and away from the crowded cargo hold. The day had been full of people talking and bustling around him. It had been draining.

He leaned a hip against the countertop in their little kitchen, stirring the gently simmering sauce. He wished his mother would let him concentrate.

"This is what you wanted, Max. You trained for it." He thought she sounded frustrated.

The timer rang, and he turned off the cooker. He poured the noodles and vegetables, picked fresh from the ship's gardens, into the sauce. Then he mixed everything gently together.

"Dinner will be ready in two minutes." He glanced at his mother's hands. There was vermiculite under her fingernails. "Wash." He pointed towards the bathroom. She tutted, but went.

He took a deep breath in the suddenly quiet room, and stared at the countertop. He counted flecks of red in the moulded plastic. Once he'd reached twenty, he started to pull out plates and cutlery, two glasses and a bottle of cold water.

"You love being out there," his mother said, coming back into the kitchen, wiping her hands on her trousers. He was tempted to tell her to wash them again, but tried to pretend he hadn't noticed. "You've wanted to work with the exterior maintenance team since you were little."

The folds around her mouth meant uncertainty, that she didn't understand.

He put on his thinking face and tried to order his thoughts. She didn't rush him. They laid the table and sat down.

He stared into his plate for a moment, then said, "I *do* want to be out there. It's beautiful. And so quiet. It's easy to focus."

"So, what's the problem, then?"

He wished she didn't sound so aggressive. It made it hard to find the words to explain.

"There's no shitguard."

"I...what?" she asked, around a mouthful of noodles.

"The EVA suits don't have shitguards to absorb cosmic radiation. The ship does. The emergency shuttles do. Even the cryosleepers have shitguards, in case of emergency evac. It's part of the waste system, but it also protects us. It's not right that the maintenance crew don't have protection." The noodles were soft and flavourful, the vegetables just slightly crunchy. He chewed, satisfied. "I don't think it's fair. I don't want to walk out into space and immediately get irradiated."

She frowned. "Have you raised it with your boss?"

"I did, yeah. He said a shitguard would make the suits too bulky." Max took another bite. It had taken a long time to get used to combined textures, but now he loved it. "I think he was blowing me off."

"Right," she said. Max waited for her annoyance to bubble over. Although she tried to stay calm, his mother often told him to stop whatabouting and just get on with things. He'd mostly stopped trying to explain that his whatabouts were important to him. "So, what are you going to do?"

He looked at her in surprise, and nearly burst into tears as a rush of gratitude welled up.

"I guess, maybe I could talk to Wayan about doing more training inside the ship. There're all sorts of internal maintenance things I don't know. Maybe I could learn more about navigation, too. I was talking to one of the trainees, Kaley, about it."

"Oh, yes?" His mother smiled.

He looked back down. "We talked. She was nice. Also, I was wondering if maybe you could show me around your lab?"

"You know I'd love to. But why?"

"Well, I have some thoughts about the EVA suits, how to develop an algae shield, maybe? Thicker cell walls or something? I thought, maybe you could help me."

His mother smiled, and reached across the table to touch his hand briefly, before he could pull away. "I'd be delighted. You know I've always wanted to get you involved in my plants."

~

FFS, Max, you can't be serious about staying. The ship will be fine by itself. It doesn't need a crew, it'll be in geosynchronous orbit. Besides, you'd be alone up here, for, like, ever.

Don't be an idiot.

Kaley

~

Max hung from the ship. He could feel the safety chord anchoring him, but otherwise he drifted in the nothingness. His comms were turned off, so he couldn't hear any chatter on the line. No one would ping him unless it was an emergency.

He stared at the planet below.

They had arrived over a month ago, spent weeks scanning, sending scouting missions, making sure the calculations from decades before were correct. His mother had gone down with one of the early groups, to start off the farms they'd need in order to support the ship's residents. Her messages sounded excited. Max missed her, but had absolutely no interest in joining. The planet looked foreign to him, and he wasn't into it. He'd been born on this ship. It was his home, and he wasn't planning to go anywhere.

He looked back at the booster he was fixing. The weld looked solid, and the readouts were good. He moved back towards the airlock.

Once inside, he drained the algae from the suit. It sloshed back into the vat, lit by growlights. He liked to think it was happy to be home after the excitement of going out.

Then he put on his headphones. The ship was busy, full of bustling people packing up their lives, getting ready to start a new one. It was noisy, chaotic. He'd taken to wearing the headphones whenever he was in the corridors, dulling the echoing noises. People assumed he was listening to something, and left him alone.

He checked his to-do list. Broken food court dispenser. Unlikely to be quiet there. Leaky sink. That'd be easy and he could lock the bathroom door. Perfect. Max turned a corner, and nearly ran into Kaley. She gestured for him to remove his headphones.

"Hey," he said.

"Jackass." It was a response, though not the one he'd hoped for. She leaned in and kissed him briefly. "You know, you wouldn't need those headphones if you just did your EVAs and then came back to my quarters."

He shrugged. "There're things to do. Plus, I won't need them when the ship is empty. When everyone else is planetside, it'll be calm. Quiet."

Kaley's face was hard to read, but he thought he detected anger. She was good at hiding her emotions, though, and he sometimes struggled to guess. He'd asked her before to tell him outright, but he wasn't sure this was the right moment to remind her.

She turned and started walking. Max decided he was supposed to follow her, so he tucked his pad into a pocket and fell into step next to her.

"You're not actually serious, right? Like, for real?" she asked.

"I mean. Yeah, I am. We've talked about this before. It's what I want to do."

"I don't get why you get to make this decision, though." She was storming down the corridor. She pushed past people, and a few of them stared after her. Max tried to look apologetic. "You're choosing for both of us. We are supposed to be partners."

Max hurried after her. "I'm sorry."

"You're sorry I'm your partner?" She took a left and opened the door to her rooms. He followed her in.

"I...no?" He paused to think, stared at a spot on the wall. "I'm sorry we want different things."

"You don't seem to care what I want. This is all about you."

Max felt this was unfair. Her perspective was all about her, after all. He had suggested that Kaley stay up here, at least for a while. She could manage the satellite launches that would support the new planet's comms system, work with the ground crew on continuing to unload the huge amounts of supplies still in storage on board. Kaley wasn't interested.

Max didn't want to have this argument again, so he shrugged.

"No one else thinks you should stay here, either. Not your mother..."

"Actually, I think she's ok with it, now she knows we can talk on messages," he said. "I got a message from her..."

"Don't interrupt me. Maybe she says it's fine, but I doubt it. And the rest of the crew think it's crazy. You're separating yourself from everyone. It's not normal." She prodded him with a finger. "Hey! Look at me when I'm talking to you."

He made eye contact for a moment, then looked away again. It was too much, trying to think and look at her.

Max wished he had the words to convince her, to convince everyone, that he was making the right decision for himself, but in the end, he didn't have to. This was what he wanted to do. It felt right to him, and they didn't have to agree.

"Look, the ship is going to be parked, but it needs someone to make sure things are ok. Like, today, I was outside, did a fix on one of the boosters, which could have died and the whole ship might have careened down to the planet. Or last week, I mended the water link to the biodome. Without it we'd have no seedbank. Or…"

"Yeah, fine, whatever." She kicked the wall, and Max briefly felt annoyed. He'd just been talking about mending the ship. He guessed that's why she'd done it.

"You could stay?" Max tried again.

"No, I couldn't." Kaley's face had gone unreadable. "And I don't want to. Everyone is going down. We're waking the last of the cryos today. It's all kicking off."

Max tried not to make a face. He wasn't looking forward to even more people bustling round the ship. At least it would be temporary.

"This is what our parents set out to do, it's what we've been raised to expect. Brave new worlds and everything. I want to be part of that." She stared at him for a moment. "You just don't get it, do you?"

Max shook his head. "No. But I don't think you get where I'm coming from, either. This is my home, it's where I belong. You know I used to get upset when they'd make us pretend to emergency evac? It's gonna be chaos down there. You say that's what you want, to be part of all that. But I don't. I want to be somewhere calm. Somewhere I feel safe. I'd like that to be with you, but if it's not…"

"Fine."

It sounded like a very final response.

"Maybe we can keep talking, though? You could tell me how it's all going down there?"

She shrugged and turned away. Max thought this was fury, though it might be sadness.

He felt sad, too. He knew it would be a lot of change for both of them. They'd been together since she'd taught him about the ship's navigation. But he hoped that she'd find new, satisfying work down on the planet, find the kind of relationship that worked for her. Because he felt good about his choice to stay and maintain the ship, and keep doing research on things that mattered to him.

His pad pinged from his pocket. He pulled it out and looked

down. Drama in the cryoroom. He looked up at Kaley, but she still had her back to him. It was a clear signal.

Max put his headphones back on, and left the room.

He would miss her. And his mother. And so many others. But, really, he was looking forward to just being here, being himself, in the deep quiet.

Heya mum,

Yep, I got the data you sent – your adapted plants are looking amazing! I've got a new strain of algae going, working on one that's transparent when it's not photosynthesising. I'll send more info soon.

Also, I've been watching the roads getting laid out from up here. NGL they don't make sense to me, but I'm sure Maresa knows what she's doing.

Had another satellite launcher failure, but it's under control now. Good times.

Love to everyone (esp. Kaley. I don't think she's ready to talk, but maybe pass it along?)

M

Emma Burnett is a neurospicy researcher and writer. She has had stories in Apex, Radon, Utopia, MetaStellar, Milk Candy Review, Elegant Literature, The Stygian Lepus, Roi Fainéant, Rejection Letters, and more. You can find her @slashnburnett, @slashnburnett.bsky.social, or emmaburnett.uk.

NEVER PICK THE BLUEBELLS

KAY HANIFEN

"It's just like a fairytale," Wendy gushed as she threw her bags onto the ancient floral couch still covered in protective plastic.

Though every part of me demanded I sleep through my jetlag, there were a few orders of business. First, I needed to turn the heat and water back on. My cousins had shut both off after Grandma died, but promised to keep paying the electricity bill until I could come to Ireland and claim my inheritance.

I didn't know why Grandma left me the cottage. I'd visited her only a couple of times, and we mostly knew each other through phone calls and video chat. I loved her, of course, but she had family here that she could have left her home to instead of a world away. But no one else seemed to resent me receiving her most valuable possession.

With my phone's flashlight on, I ventured into the cellar, trying not to think about the dust, cobwebs, and plague-carrying vermin hiding inside. My mind loves jumping to the worst-case scenario, so naturally, all the rats in the basement were carrying the Bubonic Plague. Finally reaching the dusty breaker and water main, I turned both levers while also doing my best to touch them as little as possible.

The house came to life with a sudden hum, and squirting some pocket hand sanitizer on my hands, I headed back upstairs, eager to escape the cold and dreary cellar. "We should let the water in the faucets run for a bit," I said when I got back up to the main level. "I'll do this floor if you do upstairs?"

Wendy saluted, her dark eyes sparkling. "Yes, ma'am."

Admittedly, I had an ulterior motive for sending my wife upstairs. The next order of business was the offerings. We'd stopped at the village grocery store on the way here from the airport, so I found Grandma's special teacup in the corner and poured some cream into it before topping it off with some bread.

Opening the backdoor, I set it onto the wall surrounding the patio and began putting away the rest of our groceries. Hopefully, the Good Neighbors won't give us too much trouble.

Wendy just wouldn't understand. Not really, anyway. She'd know why I felt like I had to do it and remind me of what my therapist said about breaking cycles of OCD rituals, but this was emphatically not my ridiculous brain's way of trying to control the uncontrollable through superstitions. There was a reason why Grandma had been doing this every day for as long as she'd lived in this house.

I let the kitchen and bathroom sink run until the water was clear and shut them off. Dragging our suitcases upstairs, I found Wendy looking at all the books on the Fair Folk and Celtic mythology.

She glanced over her shoulder with a smile when she heard the floor creak under my feet. "Was your grandma a professor?"

"Something like that. She was sort of an amateur folklorist," I replied, wrapping my arms around her waist, and resting my chin on her shoulder. "She'd collect the oral histories of the area—all the legends and stories from locals to make sure that they were all preserved."

Wendy stroked my hair. "She sounds pretty awesome."

"She was the best storyteller I ever knew," I said. As a child, I would sit in front of the hearth and listen enraptured as she'd tell me stories of the Dearg Due, Cú Chulainn, and Fionn mac Cumhaill's two warrior foster mothers—Bodhmall and Liath Luachra—my favorites as a queer child, though I didn't know why at the time. Even after all my cousins had wandered off to play or explore, I'd still sit at her feet listening to her stories. Maybe that was why I was given the house. She and I both understood the importance of ritual.

Unfortunately, if I really wanted to honor her memory, I was going to have to embarrass myself a little bit. Straightening, I gathered my courage. "Hey, this is going to sound weird, but there are some ground rules we should talk about before we do anything else."

Wendy turned and furrowed her brows. "Ground rules?"

"Yeah, nothing too crazy. I promise. Just don't go out at night, don't step into any mushroom circles, and make sure to wear red somewhere on your body, carry cold iron with you, and turn your clothes inside out if you get lost." I said the last few in a rush, embarrassed to have to speak these rules out loud.

"You had me for the first two, but then you lost me," Wendy said. "Are these new OCD rituals or just some that are associated with this place?"

"It's more of a cultural thing, really," I said. "Grandma made everyone follow them when they came to visit, because it's just the way things are done here. Ask anyone in town about it and they'll tell you the same."

She still was looking at me strangely, but she nodded. "Okay, that shouldn't be too hard. Thanks for telling me." Glancing over my shoulder and out the window, she asked, "Can we still go out in the daylight? I wanted to explore a bit after lunch."

I nodded. "I'd like that very much."

Rather than sleep, I had been running on willpower and a list of things that needed to be done, but as soon as I finished the spartan lunch that we'd made of grilled cheese sandwiches, the exhaustion caught up to me. I shook my head to dispel the wooziness, but that seemed to only make it worse.

"Are you sure you're up for a walk?" Wendy asked.

"Probably better if I take a nap," I replied with a yawn. "You go on ahead. Just avoid the hill to the east. The locals don't like it when people go there."

"Good to know," she replied, getting to her feet. She kissed my temple, picked up the dishes, and put them in the sink.

"Love you," I called after her as she shut the door. There was something I was forgetting. Something my sleep-deprived mind would not allow me to remember. Oh well. It'll come back to me after some sleep. Unleashing another jaw-cracking yawn, I dragged myself upstairs and took a quick shower. After blow drying my hair to make it feel less disgusting, I passed out in grandma's bed without even getting under the covers.

I woke in the late afternoon to the sound of music warbling from the kitchen. Still groggy but less dizzy, I dragged myself to my feet and down the stairs where Wendy was at work making spaghetti. A short vase filled with blue flowers sat at the center of the table. It hadn't been there when I fell asleep, and the sight of it made my body go cold. "What's that?" I asked, pointing a shaking finger at the bluebells.

"Just some wildflowers I picked," she replied, looking up from the pot. "Thought it would brighten the place up."

Of all the flowers for her to pick, it had to be bluebells, the ones the Fair Folk used to call their meetings and hang their spells. There was a reason another name for them was "Dead Man's Bells."

"We have to get rid of them," I said, my mind racing. If we'd really pissed off the Good Neighbors, there was no telling what kind of pain they would cause. But I couldn't just say that to her. She was tolerant of my rituals, encouraging me to stop them and accepting when I couldn't, but there was a difference between doing things that I know are irrational because my brain is convinced something bad will happen and saying that so-called mythical creatures are real. "They're, uh, protected. Picking them is illegal." Both those things were true and less likely to make me sound crazy.

Her eyes widened at that. "Oh, I'm so sorry. I won't do it again." Tilting her head, she added, "But what's done is done, right? I don't see any harm in keeping them around."

"It's considered very bad luck," I said. "So, please. For my peace of mind?" She knew how I felt about luck and superstitions. I always had to knock on wood when borrowing trouble and throw salt over my shoulder and hold my breath when crossing graveyards, or my brain would scream at me until another trigger came along to distract it.

But *that* was the exact wrong thing to say, because Wendy was now in *"helping her wife with exposure therapy"* mode. "Okay, how about we keep them around tonight, and if you still feel this way or something terrible happens by the morning, we can get rid of them."

Usually, I appreciated her therapy mode because it went both ways. Sometimes, her depression was so severe that she struggled to get out of bed, and I'd spend my day looking after her and whispering reassurances. We supported each other. But right now, my mind was racing with ways to appease Fair Folk and apologize for the insult.

She sighed, her shoulders sagging slightly as she shut off the stove and grabbed the vase. "Fine. I'll get rid of them." She opened the backdoor and wound up her arm to toss them out in a way that would insult the Fae even more.

"Wait!" I cried.

She paused, looking slightly irritated. "Do you want me to get rid of them or not?"

"Let me," I said, pressing a kiss to her cheek and taking the vase from her hands. I wrote *"We're sorry. Take this bread as an offering,"* on a sticky note, attached it to the vase, and grabbed one of our dinner rolls. Hopefully, that would be enough to appease them.

When I came back inside, Wendy had her arms crossed. "What was that all about?"

I threw my arm around her shoulder and said, "When in Rome..."

"You throw out flowers and bread?" she asked. Shaking her head fondly, she turned back to the kitchen, pouring out the pasta water and adding the canned tomato sauce and cheese that we'd bought. Like the grilled cheese, it was simple but made with love.

She talked about her walk while we ate, describing the sheep she saw in the fields and the locals who were fascinated by an American in this part of the world, especially an Asian American. "It was like they saw a unicorn or something," she'd said, and I struggled to tell if her laugh was genuine or strained.

Regardless, I squeezed her hand. "Tomorrow, I can show you all around town. You're gonna love it."

We stayed up only a little bit longer after that, because despite my nap, we were still exhausted, so we quickly fell back into bed.

I woke to the ringing of bells. That, in itself, wasn't unusual, because the church was nearby, but these bells were higher pitched and more musical. They were bells in the same way that a dog was a wolf.

Wendy groaned and rubbed her eyes. "What is that?" she asked.

"I-I'm not sure," I replied, opening the drawer to Grandma's night-stand, and finding exactly what I had hoped to find: a railroad spike made of cold iron. "Stay here. And don't make a sound."

"Screw that," Wendy retorted in a whisper as she followed me out of the room.

I handed her my phone with the flashlight turned on. "Don't do or say anything unless I tell you to. Understood?"

Brows furrowed in groggy confusion, she nodded, and we crept through the hall and down the stairs, wincing at every creak and groan beneath our feet. The front door had been opened, and three short men with white beards and nasty, wet red hats stood before us. Their knives glinted in the moonlight, and my mouth went dry.

Redcaps.

They were some of the nastiest Fae that my grandma would tell me about. Most Fair Folk were morally neutral, at least in the sense that they operated on a different moral logic than humanity. Though they sometimes took a prank or punishment too far, they rarely were actively malicious. Some were downright helpful. But not the Redcaps. These creatures would attack unwary travelers, soaking their hats in the blood of their victims, which allowed them to move at superhuman speeds.

"I should've known you weren't Saoirse," the Fae in the center said. "Saoirse would never have done anything so stupid."

"I would like to extend my deepest apologies," I said, stepping between them and Wendy. "It's my fault. I forgot to warn her."

He arched a scraggly eyebrow. "You take full responsibility for this insult?"

I shot Wendy a warning glare over my shoulder before saying, "I do."

"We will forgive you," he said, "but only if you play a game with us."

"What kind of game?" I reached back, taking Wendy's hand and giving it a squeeze.

"Hide and seek. We hide something precious to you in the woods, and you must find it by sunrise. If you succeed, we'll leave you be, but if you fail, we keep it," the Redcap to the right said.

"What do you want to hide?"

The one to the left smiled, revealing jagged, blackened teeth, and pointed behind me to Wendy.

I shook my head. "No. Absolutely not."

The one in the center shrugged. "I suppose that we could simply kill you both."

"I left you an offering and an apology. Don't insult me with a deal that can only ever be slanted in your favor." I slammed the door in their faces and locked it.

"What the heck?" Wendy breathed.

I grabbed her hand. "We have to move. Now." Dragging her to the kitchen, I handed her a saltshaker and grabbed one for myself. "Line the doors and windows. It'll keep them from getting in."

"What are those things?" she asked, already salting the backdoor.

"Those are fairies. Real fairies," I replied as I wracked my brain for the Redcaps' weaknesses. All Fae were vulnerable to salt and cold iron, right? Would they be forced to retreat at dawn? Or were we cornered in here until they forced us out?

"You've got to be kidding me."

"Well, you can go ahead and ask them. I'll wait," I snapped, finishing with the front door.

There was a pause. And then a quiet, "...I'm good."

"That's what I thought." I took her by the shoulders. "I'm probably going to be doing things that seem really strange to you, so I'll need you to trust that I know what I'm doing, okay?"

She straightened her back, nodding resolutely to me. We trusted one another more than anyone else in the world. Now, I just had to live up to her faith in me by getting us through this.

Grandma almost certainly had a book on Redcaps somewhere upstairs, but would I be able to find it in time? "You salt the windows upstairs while I look for a way to stop them," I said.

"Yes, ma'am."

"And put your clothes on inside out," I added as we separated in the upstairs hall. She paused, giving me a funny look, before removing her pajama shirt.

Turning my back on her, I scanned the books in Grandma's small library. Finally, tucked into a far corner, I found a book titled: *Redcaps and Other Deadly Fae of the British Isles.*

I opened it and began to skim the chapter. Like vampires, they were vulnerable to crucifixes and Bible passages. The nice thing about having a proper Irish Catholic grandma was that she had both, so I grabbed one of each. The best way to kill them, though, was to dry out their bloody hats, but good luck getting them off these creatures' heads. They were impossibly fast and immune to most human weapons. And unlike the rest of the Fae, iron didn't bother them in the slightest.

But maybe we didn't need to use a weapon. An idea formed in the back of my mind. One that might get us killed, but we'd probably die anyway. Better to go down swinging and see how many we could take with us. "Wendy," I yelled, "come here!"

We only had a few minutes to set the trap. I shut off the water and got into thicker clothes while she cranked up the heat as far as it could go. Soon, the Redcaps would get tired of waiting and attempt drastic measures to force us outside. But we weren't going outside. They were coming to us.

Standing at the front door, I waited until I heard Wendy's signal— two stomps—and broke the line of salt, opening the door for them. They all rushed in at once, and I ran upstairs.

"Where do you think you're going?" asked one as he and the other two gave chase.

I felt a sudden, sharp pain in the back of my outer thigh and stifled a cry as my leg threatened to buckle. But I kept moving, adrenaline holding the agony at bay. I didn't have to run forever—only to the upstairs bathroom. Then, I could have payback. Assuming they didn't kill me first.

Finally, I reached it, staggering to the hairdryer by the sink as they all poured in.

"Nowhere to run, nowhere to hide," the leader said.

"Exactly," I said with a smirk and then cried, "Wendy, now!" The door slammed shut. She had been hiding nearby with a string tied to the doorknob. As soon as I yelled, she pulled it closed.

I turned the hair dryer on high and full blast, turning the already warm room into a desert of dry heat. The Fae screamed and tried to pound at the door, only to be repelled by the crucifix that Wendy had nailed into it.

They turned on me, blindly slicing at my flesh while also trying to avoid the heat of the hair dryer. They were short, so it was mostly my legs that they sliced into, but it still hurt like hell even with the jeans. Luckily, they couldn't get close enough to dip their hats into my blood.

One tried to turn on the tap in the sink—probably an attempt to to prolong the hats' moisture with water—only to find that we turned off the source and emptied the pipes. As their hats began to dry to the color of rust, their flesh shriveled and crackled like fallen leaves. And then they crumpled to dust.

Not wanting to risk resurrecting them with my bloodied legs, I shut off the hair dryer and staggered into the tub. "You can open the door now," I called out.

"Christ!" Wendy exclaimed when she saw me. Damn, I must have looked really bad to get that reaction. She pulled out her phone. "I'm calling 911."

"112," I said.

She blinked. "What?"

"It's 112 in the EU." I shifted to sit up, the adrenaline crash making me feel every slash and stab. "Can you vacuum that up first? I wouldn't want to get blood on the floor and accidentally bring them back."

"They can do that?"

I shrugged, and the world seemed to be spinning on its axis a little faster than usual. "Probably. Better safe than sorry." As soon as I can, I'll vacuum it again when I'm released from the hospital. And maybe a third time, just to be safe. Three was a nice number. I always liked to do things in threes.

Wendy snapped in my face. "Hey, where's the vacuum cleaner?"

"Laundry room," I replied, drifting for a bit until someone began to move my legs. I stifled a cry.

"Sorry, sorry," Wendy said, "but I can't let you bleed out. The ambulance is on their way."

"Did you vacuum?" I asked.

She snorted. "Went over the area twice and laid down a towel on top. You don't have to worry about accidentally bringing them back." Biting her lip, she pressed a kiss to my forehead. "I'm so sorry you got hurt because of me."

I shook my head. "Hey, it was my plan. And I didn't warn you enough."

She sighed. "I doubt I would have believed it even if you did. I'm sorry about that too."

"At any other time, you'd be right," I replied, feeling the familiar itch in the back of my brain. What if I'd already spilled blood on the ashes and the Redcaps would resurrect at any moment? "But I appreciate your apology."

There was a knock at the door, and she disappeared to let the paramedics in. As they lifted me out of the bathtub, one asked, "What happened?"

"Word of advice," I replied through gritted teeth as they laid me onto the stretcher. Wendy took my hand, and I gave it a squeeze. *"Never pick the bluebells."*

Kay Hanifen was born on a Friday the 13th and once lived for three months in a haunted castle. So, obviously, she had to become a horror writer. Her work has appeared in over forty anthologies and magazines. When she's not consuming pop culture with the voraciousness of a vampire at a 24-hour blood bank, you can usually find her with her two black cats or at kayhanifenauthor.wordpress.com.

Twitter: https://twitter.com/TheUnicornComi1

Instagram: https://www.instagram.com/katharinehanifen/

ALL IN MY HEAD

GERRI LEEN

I wake. It's dark, not dark as in almost sunrise, but dark as in I slept through the day again and now it's night. I'm still tired and wonder what woke me as I light the oil lamp. Hunter and Casper are sprawled lengthwise on the bed as cats like to do—I've slept in a sort of "Z" pattern to not disturb them. My neck is killing me but I don't know if it's because of the contortions or just the migraine.

I slip on my glasses and look for the dogs. Jax and Jake are awake on the floor and looking at me expectantly. Zingo's nowhere to be seen. Then I hear him bark, out in the main room.

I wonder if it's Cam at the door. With one of her annoying questionnaires or new ways to test my loyalty to the community. It would piss me off if I didn't know she does it to everyone.

If I didn't know how much she gives and will always give to us, to keep us safe and prospering.

Zingo's bark changes to the three-bark pattern that means someone he likes is at the door. Can't be Cam then.

I throw the covers off, tell Jake and Jax to stay, shove feet into clogs, and get up, taking three steps before I realize how dizzy I am.

Hunter chirps. My little assistance cat, even if he's not very helpful in the assisting part. His ability to comment on my state of health is first rate though.

"Yes, I know I'm sick today. Unless you want to go get the door, I still need to get up."

Sick. Some might think I'm always sick. Migraine is funny that way. I'm always feeling it—there's never a day I'm not affected in some way. But I don't always think of myself as sick. Just on the days where the bad episodes come. The headache—or the vertigo like now, which can be so much worse. The days all I can do is sleep. The days I don't sleep, infused instead with a manic energy. And if it's at night, well, that's fine. I can walk the dogs—get training done. But in the day? If it's too bright?

I used to have prescription sunglasses. They got lost or stolen during the worst of the Crisis. Newcomers have brought some in with them since then, but they're never the right strength. So I have to sit out the manic jags inside, pacing, wondering what the hell to do with no devices or television. Too agitated to just sit and read.

Feeling that familiar panic when I feel good, when I feel not sick. Like my body's saying, "Let me *do* something." Until it remembers that doing something is great so long as it's not too bright or too loud or too smelly.

Migraine: a brain wired wrong. That was the conclusion my neurologists had come to before the Crisis came. Before people worrying about universal healthcare gave way to worrying about if there was even a doctor within a day or two's walk.

Now there is. Now that Leanna moved in. Communities fought for her: we offered the best incentives. She's a general physician, but she saw enough migraine patients to know what might help me—if what might help me was made anymore. Which it isn't. Or if it is, it isn't trickling down to us yet.

So I muddle through. And on days like this, when the vertigo is so bad I feel as though I've gotten off the cup ride at an old-time carnival, then I feel sick. The other days—well, after the Crisis, who the hell doesn't have a hard time?

At least I'm safe and warm, with shelter and food and a community.

I maneuver to the front door and open it to see Daniel standing outside.

He doesn't say hello. Doesn't ask me how I am. Just studies me for a moment and then says, "Bad night, Manda?"

"Dizzy."

"Sucks."

"Does."

We've perfected this verbal shorthand over time. I smile, the best smile I can, and he gives me the same kind back. We've been doing some kind of dance around each other for a while now. I used to think I was good at this—relationship stuff, attraction. But being sick made me forget. Disability mercifully let me not work, but then I was stuck in my house. With little interaction on most da

Until the Crisis. Irony: most people became less sociable during it. I became more.

"You're back." I'm trying to dial back the stupidly large grin I've got going, but I've missed him. He's been gone two weeks.

"I am." He leans up against the door and seems to relax as Zingo demands pets. "Heard this guy going nuts. So I'm a three-bark person now?"

I laugh. "Don't let it go to your head. Labradors are easy graders."

He crouches down and looks past me. "But pitties aren't. Jake, come here, boy."

Jake, as always, rushes him, covering him with big, slobbery pit-bull kisses.

"I didn't release him, Daniel."

"I did. And he's gonna be my dog. Isn't that what you said?"

I roll my eyes.

"What? You're gonna change your mind now? Might want to wait till you see what I have in the back." He points to the cart he drags behind his bicycle. His grin tells me everything.

Then I hear the mews.

"You found some?"

Jake is already heading over to the cart, tail up in a way I'm not loving. "Jake, down," I say, not bothering to see if he's dropped as I pass him.

He's a good dog. He always drops. Except when Daniel's calling him. Truth is he's always been Daniel's dog; it just took us all a while to know it.

And while Jake is fully trained, Daniel isn't. So I'll hold on to Jake just a bit more until I'm sure the two of them can work as a seamless team.

But good as he is, the last thing I want is for Jake to meet the kittens before I do. They're in a basket, under a towel and there are four of them and a mama cat who hisses at me as I lift the cover up. I don't try to pet her, just study her, blinking slowly and talking low, the way the cat I had before the Crisis used to like.

It takes a while, but finally she gives me a grudging slow-blink back. Her pupils aren't as big so I reach carefully and pick up the basket. "I love you, Daniel."

"Yeah, you say that now." He steadies me as the world spins a bit when I straighten up. "You want me to carry that?"

I think about it. It's stupid not to consider his offer. I don't want to hurt the kittens because I'm too proud to ask for help. But the dizziness subsides and I say, "No, I got it."

He goes on as if I never had a problem. "She did *not* want to come. Till I gave her some of those treats you make."

"You used the gloves?" Cat scratches and bites get infected fast.

"Yep. I do listen to you, Manda."

Laughing, I take a step toward the house, then turn to study the cart. It's unusually full. "What is all this?"

"My stuff."

"Why?"

"We're getting some engineers. Both of them have families. So I'm giving up my house."

"That's big of you."

"Hey, Cam says they can get the grid working. If that's true, even a little, it's worth it."

"There are other houses. You're the last person who needs to be tested for loyalty."

"Cam's rules." He shrugs. He doesn't tend to badmouth Cam, and I sort of love that about him. He doesn't care if I do, though. In fact, I think he finds it cathartic.

"Yeah, but the dorms." I make a face because I'm not really a people person and neither is he—it's why he loves being on patrol, going off for weeks exploring and finding all kinds of things for the community as well as cats and dogs for me to gentle. I'm hoping some day he brings us a horse, but any that got loose were snatched up early by the country folks. We're too suburban to have farms nearby.

But plenty of dogs and cats. So many during the Crisis were left in houses to starve when it would have been kinder to let them go feral. We didn't get to them all in time, and it broke my heart every time we buried any. But we helped enough of them to start breeding them, to use the trained dogs and the good mouser cats for our own needs and later for barter, and I rehabbed the first of them. Still do the hard dogs and cats. But we've got regular fosters now for the low-mainte-nance ones. A whole system I'm in charge of.

And not just because we love animals and they make us feel good. They're damned useful. Guarding things, working sentry duty, hauling stuff, pest control. And hunting.

And I can be useful too when I help this way. I can give back. No one has my touch with a scared animal. Not saying that to boast. Kind of the opposite. I know what it's like to be overwhelmed by stimulus others find normal. To not feel like you fit in.

To be scared you might get thrown out.

To be grateful when you're not and determined to give back.

That's how the animals seem to me.

I take the cats in and put the basket in my room, in the closet I've used for the nursing litters. One the dogs aren't allowed in. I imagine it smells like cats and safety and happy families to the mama cat. It might also smell like not so happy moments—not all the litters come in healthy—but this mama's been in the world. She knows what it's like.

I realize Daniel's behind me.

"She looks happy." He touches my shoulder gently and I wonder, not for the first time, what it would be like to be with him. Happy and together.

But who the hell wants to live life like I do? Crazy hours. Me always dizzy or hurting. Focused on myself, living inside my own head so much of the time that I can't see out.

And avoiding the sun like I'm some sort of vampire? Can't see that being a great enticement. Can't see him running to put my name down in the "Pick me" contest that is courtship these days.

And one neurologist told me migraine's hereditary. A genetic lottery winner I'm not.

Then again, everyone's usually got something wrong. Some just hide it better.

Or at least that's what I tell myself when I'm determined to find the silver lining. Usually when I'm thinking about Daniel.

"The dorm's horrible," I say it before I can think. "Stay here." Then I close my eyes and wish my stupid mouth would coordinate better with my brain.

But it's out and his grasp on my shoulder tightens. "Here?"

"I mean, I've got the spare room. I'd rather have you in it than Cam assigning some random person—you know she'll pick someone who'll irritate the crap out of me just for grins. And you like the animals. Aren't allergic or anything." I can't look at him. Can't let him see I'm dying of embarrassment that I've asked—but also don't want him to know how much I want him to say yes. "But you might prefer the dorm. Be with the guys. I mean, I know this isn't a very exciting place and—"

"Yes."

"Yes?"

"Yeah, that'd be great." His grip lets up, but he doesn't pull away. "Really, really great."

"Jake'll be ecstatic."

"Just Jake?"

The humor I love is back in his voice. "Okay, Zingo may also be very happy."

He laughs and says, "And you won't be?"

"Well, maybe a little." He helps me up in a way that isn't annoying, just nice, not pitying, and we head out to the main room.

"Sit down before you fall down. I'm gonna start moving my stuff in."

We share a long look, then I sit down and Zingo and Jake jump up the couch with me, licking me like it's their birthday or something as they watch him go back and forth from the cart to the spare room.

I imagine the dogs are a little bored with just me.

Hunter and Casper, on the other hand, are standing in my bedroom doorway looking at me like I've betrayed them. First another set of kittens and a bitchy-ass mama cat and now a new human?

I can tell they think I suck.

Jax is off by himself, twirling. I need to figure a way to get him to stop doing that when he's excited and nervous. It's a little obsessive— or maybe I just don't get why he'd want to be dizzy if he could help it.

God knows I'd happily never feel this way again.

"Jax," I say, and give the short, sharp whistle that's his.

He's part Border Collie—I think. He's black and white, and has the herding look and eye. And he perks up at the whistle. He's dancing as he watches me. Like me in one of my manic periods— stuck in this damned house.

I get up and Daniel glares at me as he mutters, "Can't you just sit?"

"Jax is coming out of his skin. Gonna play a bit while the moon's out. Let you and the mama cat convince the terrible two over there"— I gesture at Hunter and Casper—"that you moving in here is a good idea."

"Oh sure, leave me with the hard work." But he grins because even if Hunter isn't that fond of him, Casper has been known to cuddle with him a time or two when Daniel and I have sat up late, talking into the morning while the rest of the community—except the sentries—slept.

It's one of the reasons I trust him. Because the animals love him.

"All right, doggos. Let's go," I say.

All three are at my side, but Jake whimpers as I make him leave Daniel. He chases the ball a few times, clearly not into it, and I finally let him go back to the house.

Zingo and Jax, though, are all in, and I hold onto the picnic table as I heave the ball for them. The world spins but the nighttime seems soft and welcoming, and behind me I can hear Daniel talking to the cats and the raspy cry that can only be Hunter giving him backtalk.

It's a weird life, but it's mine. And his, too, now. Well, sort of. Sharing space isn't a commitment, but it's something more than I had before. Even if I know he'll be gone a lot.

I hear his steps coming—when did I memorize the cadence, the way he favors one leg a little?

"You okay?" He touches my hand where I'm holding on to the table.

"Just dizzy. Same old same old."

"Sucks."

"Does."

We both laugh softly. This ritual is comforting even if it's bleak.

"Oh, crap. I can't believe I forgot." He hurries to his cart, starts digging around in the part that's not his stuff, and then comes back with a bottle. "This is what you used to take, isn't it?"

He shines his flashlight on the label long enough for me to see what it is. Codeine.

"That'll help you, right?"

I swallow hard. It will help me. So, so much. For a moment, I just clutch the bottle, remembering how many times I sucked down these pills—none of the new drugs worked for me so my doctor went old school, willing to let me have these so long as I watched my intake. I can almost feel how blissful the temporary relief was when my head felt like it was going to pound off my neck.

But it was always temporary.

I shake the bottle. So many pills.

So many respites: temporary or not, they still felt so good.

I want to keep them. I want to take them and hide them somewhere no one but me can ever find them.

Instead, I press them into his hands and meet his eyes and try to make sure he can tell I'm serious when I say, "Give them to Leanna. She might need them for a real emergency."

"You sure? They can help you, right?" He holds them back out.

I nod but don't reach for them.

His smile's luminous, and he eases me to him, really slow, like he wants me to be able to pull away if I don't want the same thing he does. And then we're kissing, and his mouth is warm and firm but not too firm. Just right.

When we finally pull away, he buries his face in my hair, his lips near my ear, and whispers, "I told Cam you'd choose right."

"This was a test?" Crud, I must be slipping. I'm usually wise to her tricks.

And man does she know my Kryptonite.

Only not. Because I gave the pills back.

"Yeah. A test. Just like giving up my house was one for me—you weren't wrong. Cam sure does love her tests."

"You know she wants a cat, right? She'll be waiting a while."

"Fine by me." He pulls me back to him, and we kiss some more and even though I'm ticked off, it's hard to be really pissed at Cam if kissing Daniel is my reward for passing her stupid loyalty test.

We finally pull away and he says, "That's nice. I thought it would be."

"Yeah?"

He nods.

"It is nice. Really, really nice. Maybe Cam'll get a cat after all. Maybe from this litter you just got me."

His laugh is hearty and makes me feel the way I always do when I take him by surprise with my humor. Like I'm secure and strong and...healthy. Like there's not a thing in the world wrong with me.

"Hey, I really did find something for you. And Cam can't say a damn thing because this will let you go out in the day and spend more hours training the pups."

"For the community," we say together, intoning the words like brainwashed cult members. An old joke we both think is way funnier than anyone else seems to.

He takes my hand, as if he doesn't want to let go of me, and leads me to the cart. He digs around again, then hands me an oversized eyeglass case. "These go over your glasses. So you don't need special prescription ones."

I open it and try the huge sun-shades on over my glasses. A perfect fit. And they are so dark I can barely see. "Oh, Daniel. You don't know..." I swallow hard and this time it's not because I'm making a hard choice. This time it's so I won't cry.

He gives me the moment to get myself together. Then he says softly. "You can go out in the day now, when it's bright. I don't know if you know how much your hair shines in the sun." He adjusts the glasses gently, in a way that's possessive, but in a good way. "They look nice on you."

"No they don't."

"Well, you make them look nice—how's that?" His smile is easy, as if this is just a fact for him. But then he gets serious as he eases them off and puts them back in the case. "Am I assuming anything here, Manda? I mean, I've kind of had a plan, I'll admit it. But that's maybe not fair to you. So if I am assuming, I can go to the dorm."

"You're not assuming anything I don't want you to assume." I cup his cheek. "But...can we take our time? You don't know what it's like, what I'm like, when I'm really sick."

"Okay. And anytime you need space, just say so. I'll give it to you."

"And if I don't need space?"

His smile is so silly it makes me giggle—how long has it been since I've done that? "Well, that's all right too."

I realize the dogs are dancing around us, even Jake.

"Throw the damn ball, so we can get back to kissing."

"Throw it yourself. I'm not doing all the work around here."

"Oh yeah, I see. I see how it's gonna be." He's talking to Jake but glancing back at me, an even sillier grin on his face.

I feel dizzy, and I'm not sure if it's the migraine or love.

Either way, it's okay.

Gerri Leen lives in Northern Virginia and originally hails from Seattle. During her not insignificant amount of years on this planet, she has watched her episodic migraine become more severe, then turn chronic and manifest as vestibular in addition to classic. When one of many neurologists explained that migraine brains are wired differently than normal, all those times she was overly sensitive to light, sound, smell, taste, and even texture became so much more understandable. She has stories and poems in The Magazine of Fantasy & Science Fiction, Nature, Strange Horizons, Dark Matter and others, and is a member of SFWA and HWA. See more at gerrileen.com.

A PLACE TO BELONG

R.B. KELLY

Every day I weave the curtain, and every evening I go back and unpick the work I've done. Not so much as to be noticeable – just enough and no more.

Jana sits near me in the orchard as I weave. She doesn't talk and neither do I. The old curtain stretches above us and the light that filters through is a rich emerald green, scattered through with black patches of shadow where the holes have been covered. In the soft hush that surrounds us, I imagine I can hear the whisper of photo-electric current in the tendrils that open onto the unfiltered sky above. There's life in the curtain yet, despite its age. Power enough for now.

I'm here to weave a replacement because *for now* is running short.

As the sun crawls high above us and the deep jade light of morning begins to yellow and turn golden, the scents of cooking stretch and curl among the apple trees. Corn bread. Baked squash. Something sharp with basil. Jana dims the screen of her notepad, stretches her shoulders and sucks in a deep breath that sets her scarred lungs coughing. She grins, the smile of a much younger woman, and says, "Lunch?"

"In a minute," I say. I know by now I don't need to meet her eye. "I'll finish this line and then I'll come."

She nods and eases herself up off her stool. Her bones unfold like the spines of an unravelling basket. She puts one hand to her back where the ache has set in from sitting, and says, "I'll save you a bowl."

I watch her go, collecting others as she passes from their pruning, their weeding, their lessons. I listen to the soft fade of their voices as they head toward the rec building, the rush of conversation that explodes from the building as the doors swing open. The sudden silence as they swing closed again. Fat spots of water drop from the branches and the leaves, finding irrigation channels in the soil, and bees croon as they scatter to and from the hives. I'm alone. Unseen.I hum to myself as I set to unstitching a few threads before anyone thinks to come looking for me.

When I first arrived at the settlement, the questions were like a wall.

Are you really from outer space? the children wanted to know, and the adults, who knew where I'd come from, were burning with curiosity about the sensation of terrestrial gravity after a lifetime of centrifugal force on the annulets, about the taste of coffee and chocolate and the way coconut smells. About how it feels to stand by a window and gaze out into the void.

I don't know that I ever answered to their satisfaction. They don't ask me anymore.

As dusk falls, I carefully spool the curtain so that the strands won't snag, and I wrap it in damp silk cloth to keep the algal fibres moist. In my mind's eye, I'm sketching how it will look when I've finished tonight's unravelling: no more than three lines, I think. I lift it carefully, and it feels like downy feathers beneath my fingers as I carry it to the rec building.

The evening meal is almost over and an air of lethargy has settled over the communal areas. Jana sits by the empty fireplace with her partner, Ursula, and Felix, their middle son. Jana's eyes are closed so she doesn't see me, but Ursula does and she smiles warmly. Felix doesn't look up from his book, but then again, he rarely does.

I take my dinner onto the upper terrace, where the groups of people are thinnest of all and I can be alone. Above me, stars prickle through the night-time haze. Brightest among them are the annulets: seventeen ring cities, locked in a perpetual mid-Earth orbit.

My home.

Regulus Sector 7 will be online by now, I think. It's hard to visualise it clearly anymore, though it's less than six months since I left. I've woven curtains for three of those seven sectors. In cavernous, echoing bays, I've sat and twisted fine strands of bio-voltaic thread into the mesh that powers worlds. It was my mother's idea, not my father's, but by then he understood I'd never manage in the control rooms.

"They brought us here," he would tell me often, "and they can send us away just as easily."

For the longest time, I feared he was right.

"Is it possible," Jana asks, "to refine the weave so we can use it for climate control?"

She's worried about the cereal crop. It's been too long since the last rainfall and there's not enough spare water to keep the maize from wilting.

I don't look up from what I'm doing. "With the weave alone? No," I say. "It's not designed for that."

She makes a noise in the back of her nose. "What if it was doubled up?"

I try to picture what I think she's asking. It makes no sense. "The top layer of the curtain would collect solar energy," I say. "The bottom would be useless. If you want extra shade for the growing fields, you'd be better off with just regular cloth. Thin, maybe."

She makes the noise again. "I don't know if that would work."

Neither do I. I'm not a farmer. My anxiety rises and I shake my head to clear it.

"I should let you get back to your weaving," Jana says, but she doesn't go. Instead, she reaches out her arm to brush her hands through the sagging crop stems. They rustle wetly together, dampened by the mister, and some broken-off bits of seed cling to her fingers.

I turn to my half-formed curtain. I weave a loop, then a whorl. My skin is green between the ridges of my fingerprints to a depth that never scrubs out. It used to bother me, but now my hands would look wrong without it.

"Well," Jana says, "we won't starve if we lose this one harvest. But people do love their baking. Perhaps we can divert some of the stored water from the shower units...?"

That would work. It would also lower the power consumption in that section of the settlement, which will probably help.

"We wouldn't have to go completely without," she says. "Maybe ration it down to... I don't know, once a week? Would that be more or less popular than a lost corn harvest, though? Oh, I don't know..."

It sounds as though she's talking to herself, so I'm not sure why she's still here. Anxiety buzzes like restless insects inside my skull and I shake my head again to quiet them. As if she's finally noticed me, Jana turns her head towards me and flashes a tight, warm smile. "Sorry," she says. "Not your problem. Ignore me, Laura; sorry. Are you comfortable? Do you have everything you need?"

I do, but the sound of her words have started to turn white-hot. A hum rises in my throat and my body moves in time with the sound, soothing me. Blocking out the world.

"Sorry," she says again. "I'll leave you to your weaving." Before silence can descend, she adds, quickly, "We're lucky to have you. I just wanted you to know that we know that."

We'll be lucky if they don't put us on the next transport back to Earth, spits my father's voice out of my memory. I hum a little more loudly to drown him out.

When I open my eyes again, Jana is gone.

In its current state of repair, I estimate the curtain can pull enough power to last three more seasons. I can't drag out my work as long as that, so I'll be finished long before it fails. This still buys me a little more time before I have to go back.

Everyone wins this way.

In the solitude of my room, I unpick six rows of today's weave. It's delicate work. I don't want to damage the threads or there's a chance the whole curtain will fail when it's connected to the grid, but my hands know this fabric as well as the clothes on my back and I'm patient, unhurried.

Outside my open window, the settlement is quiet. A baby fusses somewhere. Hushed laughter scatters from late-night conversations. Clicks and hisses follow the mister as it changes course along the tracks that carry it through the gardens. Pipes and heat sinks rumble underground – noise that's barely noise at all.

I never realised until I arrived here how relentless of an assault the noise was back home.

As a child, my bedtime stories were about the withering, hopeless world beneath us. My parents agreed on very little, but one thing they did was that the only future for us was on the annulets.

They brought us here. It's as though my father engraved his words on my bones. *They can send us away just as easily.*

He hoped I'd follow him into general operations. But everyone talks to everyone all the time in the control rooms: a hundred conversations all flying through the air like bullets, and the cannon roar of machinery wrestles with the rattle of vehicles and the electric fizz of circuitry until the whole place seems to burn with the force of its own disorder. Even my humming can't silence a roar of chaos like that. It was clear by day three I wouldn't last in the job he found for me. I'm lucky my mother was able to apprentice me to the weavers.

Twenty-two years later, when they told me I was being sent to repair a deteriorating curtain on the blue-smudged world below, I thought I'd finally run out of chances. I begged them to assign someone else. It never crossed my mind, when I arrived here at Jana's settlement, that I'd come to find myself so terrified of leaving it.

～

Through the habit of a lifetime, I'm awake before dawn. Early morning is my time, and I've come to understand that I need its stillness to armour me against the day ahead.

This morning is different. I know this before I see the figures standing in a field that should be deserted for at least another hour. At first, I'm not sure how I know it. The wrongness of difference shouts down the question inside the sudden tumble of my thoughts. So it's a full thirty seconds before I register the greater error that looms over the presence of Jana, Christophe and Arielle in the pre-dawn garden.

The air is dry. The mister has stopped working.

～

The aridity alarm woke her in the small hours, Jana explains. Her eyes are pink with lack of sleep and her skin sags around her jaw.

"Looks like there was a power dip in two out of three of the capacitor modules," Christophe says. His hand rasps over his stubbled chin. "The third's still got some juice but it wasn't enough to get the pump up to pressure."

"What about the auxiliaries?" I ask.

He shrugs. "We've been playing for time for...a while now."

Arielle, his dayshift counterpart, adds, "We haven't had the spare capacity to let the auxiliaries charge. It's all been going to the primaries."

Shame spikes my belly, though I know this wasn't because of me. Even if I'd been working honestly, the curtain wouldn't be finished yet, and I didn't know how badly their power storage had decayed.

"My fault," Jana says, as though I've spoken my thoughts out loud.

"I've been rationing the water supplies, and I've clearly spread them too thin. If the tank had been full, the extra pressure might have…"

Arielle puts a hand around Jana's arm. "You can't make it rain," she says.

∻

I can't bring myself to unpick the weave tonight.

My hands are clumsy today. I've barely finished five full rows by the time exhaustion spears my eyes and I look up to see the sun has almost set already. I close my eyes and press my thumb and forefinger against my eyelids, creating white spots to fill the darkness. Outside my window, the settlement is winding down towards night-time, and the voices that filter up to my second storey room are soft. Beneath them, around them, are the sounds of perpetual industry, the heartbeat of this village: creaks, hisses, deep rumbles and sighs. Noise but not noise. So different from home.

Home.

I don't know how I'll ever go back to it, now that I know how silence feels.

I've been wetting my hands as I work, flicking beads of water from my fingers to keep the algal strands from drying out. Still, the fabric feels brittle beneath my touch as I carefully roll it up and slide it into the silk holder. At home, the weaving rooms are bathed in a constant 75% humidity and sometimes I'd feel as though I was drowning after a 10-hour shift, but it made for beautiful curtains.

At home.

I must get used to thinking of it that way again.

∻

"It's not your fault," Jana says, as though she's been reading my restless thoughts. I shake my head a little to clear away the lingering trace of unease, and I drop my eyes back to the threads.

If she was surprised to find me here, weaving by starlight on the rec's upper terrace, she's given no sign. And, though I'd prefer to work alone, it isn't exactly a revelation that she's as sleepless as I am tonight. I don't like this change to my routine, but I don't like the way the sun's dried the fibres either in the absence of the misters, and there are compensations for keeping unsociable hours.

At least, there would be, if Jana were able to sleep.

I hum softly in the back of my throat. Jana doesn't expect an answer and I don't try to find one. It's hard enough without breaking my concentration to see the stitches in this light.

"We won't lose the crop," she says now. "If you were worrying about that. We won't. I mean...it'll be more effort to water the gardens by hand, but we've done it before."

I nod. I don't lift my eyes. The silence lengthens, and usually she's fine to let it stretch between us, but it seems that, tonight, she needs to talk. She sucks in a deep breath, lets it out slowly, and says, "I simply can't imagine the curtains on your home. I've tried – I just... can't. For me, they're just part of the gardens. Woven into them, like they're growing from the plants beneath. They're living things, aren't they? Of a kind? I can't imagine them on a world of metal and plastic."

"There are gardens on the annulets," I say. I don't add that our miles upon miles of greenery would dwarf this little settlement by a factor of thousands. Jana already knows this.

"Of course," she says. "But they're not quite the same, are they?"

It takes me a minute to work out what she might mean. "Some of the parkland is given over to farming."

"True." She waves a hand. "Oh, never mind me. Too many years of soil chemistry and water tables and mycorrhiza. Tell me about your gardens."

They're not *my* gardens, I want to say, but it feels too defensive. So I default to science and statistics: the plants that do well in centrifugal gravity and the plants that don't, the complicated balance of hydrology and oxygen management, and the trade-off between power capture and the ferocity of our naked sun.

"There's no scientific reason," I say, "for your curtains to hang over the growing fields. That's how we do it on the annulets because the gardens are the only part of the habitat with a UV-permeable wall. But down here... you could hang your curtains anywhere you like."

Jana says nothing for a moment, and belatedly I realise I've just given detailed answers to a lot of questions she didn't ask. This is why I prefer not to talk at all. But then a slow smile eases the lines around her eyes, and I wonder if perhaps I haven't done as badly as I think.

"It seems to me," she says, "that we've hung our curtains exactly right, though. Wouldn't you agree?"

I open my mouth to tell her that's exactly what I've been trying to explain, but I catch myself in time. "You should hang them where you like," I say instead. "It won't change their effectiveness."

This is almost certainly the wrong way to reply, I realise a half-second after the words leave my mouth. Jana's face betrays a flash of something that looks, for an instant, as though I've just sworn at her, but then it's gone and she smiles again.

"That," she says, "is why we need you."

I weave all night, long after exhaustion finally sinks its claws into Jana's shoulders and harries her off to bed. I weave by the thin light of the solar lamps and then by the thin light of the creeping dawn. By the time Karol arrives to start breakfast, the sky is grey and the earth-bound lights of the annulets have vanished like smoke into mist, and I'm still weaving.

He nods at the curtain in my hands as he wipes beads of dew from the balcony tables and into the collection tub he carries. "That's looking good."

I say nothing, just hum quietly, and don't stop what I'm doing. The humming creates a comfortable vibration in my skull, which is thick with sleeplessness

When the rec begins to fill with hungry bodies, I wrap my filigree strands carefully into their dampened silk holder and slip quietly past the queues. I return to my room with a head full of noise and lie on the bed with my eyes closed for the count of ten, twenty, thirty. It's no good. Daylight is not the time for sleeping, and I have work to do.

It's cooler in my room than in the un-misted gardens. The air is dry, but the shadows are long. I wet my hands with water from yesterday's rations, and I weave.

Night has fully fallen before I notice that the day has disappeared. My hands are thick and stiff with use as I lean back, stretch out the burning ache in my shoulders. The room is cool. The pangs from my empty stomach fade into background noise.

I survey the product of the past long hours. Ripples of emerald green cascade across the floor. Outside, a gaggle of voices spears the air with laughter, carried on the fumes of a dinner just past, and my head, which has been blissfully empty all day, starts to spin.

I drop back onto my pillow, close my eyes. Count to ten, to twenty, to thirty. Sleep tugs at me from the darkness and I feel it fuzzing the edges of my skull. But beneath it is a riptide of restless energy, of *need*, that is stronger by far.

I sit up slowly. My eyesight wobbles but the world holds firm. I've woven through longer stretches than this before.

They brought us here and they can send us away just as easily.

I don't want to go back to the annulets. I don't want to go back to hoarding stolen moments of quiet and feeling as though I'm never more than a couple of seconds away from fracturing, as though there's something inside me always ready to break. I don't want to shrug back into that shell I pieced together to look like a working version of me, just to face each day.

I don't want to go back, but I don't belong here. I have a job to do, and I haven't done it, and that has caused this settlement harm.

I don't want to cause them harm.

I crack my knuckles and get back to work.

When I open my eyes, the room is different.

Jana is here, sitting in an old wicker chair that's not part of my furniture. Something is beeping somewhere, and there's a person on the far side of the room that I've never seen before. My adrenaline spikes and beeping picks up to the pace of my racing heart.

The new person turns and smiles as though we're old friends. "Well, hello there," he says. "Welcome back to the land of the living."

He's a doctor, I realise. The beeping is from a heart monitor at the foot of the bed.

In some buried place, I feel a hum try to rise, but it feels like there's a strong weight holding it down. This should be more worrying than it is.

"You collapsed," Jana says quietly. "When we didn't see you at breakfast... Rana found you on the floor in your room. You were still holding the threads of the curtain."

"Oh," I say. I hope I haven't damaged the weave.

"Laura..." she says, and trails off. Then: "What were you thinking?"

I don't understand the question. "I was trying to see how quickly I could replace..."

"Yes. I know." Her tone is sharp. Nothing makes sense to me right now. "I told you we could water the crops. You didn't need to... to do *this* to yourself."

There's no doctor in the settlement. This knowledge filters through belatedly. They'll have had to send out for someone to care for me, and the power drain of my life support will drop the feed to the gardens even lower.

"I need to finish the curtain," I say, though I can hardly lift my arms off the sheet, so I'm not sure how that's going to happen.

There's a short pause. Then Jana glances up at the doctor and flashes one of her smiles. "Could you give us a minute?"

He nods. "Of course. I'll get us some tea, shall I?"

"Lovely. Thank you." Jana's smile holds in place as her eyes follow him across the few short steps to the door, and he nods once, briefly, before stepping through and closing it behind him. She lets the silence hang for a moment as his footsteps retreat down the corridor outside, and then a moment longer. Finally, she says, "I told your mother I'd keep an eye on you, you know."

This is news to me. "I didn't know you knew my mother."

"We were offered a place on Sirius 2 when our children were small," Jana says. The non sequitur makes my bones itch. "Have I ever told you that?"

I assume she knows perfectly well that she hasn't. I wait for her to continue.

"That was... oh, I think eight or nine years before we had the chance to set up here. So we had no idea what the future held back then. Nobody did. We didn't even know if there'd *be* a future. Ursula and I – we talked, and talked, and worried, and went round and round in circles – were we crazy, were we fools, were we dooming our family – yes, it was as bad as that. You don't remember, I expect, because you were so young – hardly even two years old, weren't you, when your family emigrated? But... yes. It was as bad as that."

She's taken the band of her cardigan between the long fingers of both hands and she rubs the wool as though she's trying to scrub out a stain.

"You see," she says slowly, "I'd visited Sirius 1 not too many years before. It was about... thirty percent online then?" This sounds like a question, but she carries on before I can answer. "All those people. And none of them were starving. None of them were homeless. Everyone had a job. Families had proper, multi-room units, just for themselves. There were communities – proper communities. With cook-outs in the park. Little League teams. Choirs. Choirs!" She breaks off with a small laugh, as though collective song is the most incredible feature of annular life. "It was everything I remember from my childhood. Cinemas. Theatres, shopping malls – whole districts of them in some sectors. Schools. All those things I used to take for granted... and there they were. I mean, yes, of course there were sacrifices. But there are always sacrifices, aren't there? And there they were, offering me a job. A home. A *future*."

It's no surprise the annulets would have sought out someone like Jana at the peak of her former career. But the pause continues long enough that I understand something's expected of me, so I say, "But you didn't accept."

She smiles. She doesn't lift her eyes. "How could I?"

It takes me a moment. Part of that is whatever the doctor has given me, I think, fogging my brain. Part of it is because there's quite a large semantic leap required. But then some weary neuron fires an image of her son Felix across my mind's eye, and I suddenly understand.

At least I think I do. "Oh," I say.

Jana nods, slowly. This makes me more confident my instinct is right. "Ask me," she says, "if I've ever regretted that decision."

"Did you?" I whisper. My mouth feels dry.

Her response is fierce and immediate. "Never."

"Even when..." I have to ask. I don't think I have the words, but I have to ask, so I try again. "Even when..."

She glances up, doesn't quite meet my eye. Glances down again. "There were bad years down here," she says softly. "But can you honestly tell me that there were no bad years up there?"

And I think of my mother, the way she'd look at my father sometimes. The way the walls in our pod were never thick enough, and the way she'd struggle to keep her voice down as she tried to explain, over and over. The way she'd just stopped going out, after a while. The way he eventually stopped asking.

"Look," Jana says. "We never imagined that we could keep you here. I know your skills are in demand back on Regulus. But... our curtains are old. All of them. They're worn down and they're starting to fail. I mean... we can patch them up if we need to. But... if you'd consider... if we could persuade you to stay..."

She trails off so gently that it's a couple of seconds before I realise she's stopped speaking. It's a couple more before I go back over what she's just said and understand what she's offering.

"I... thought the settlement was at capacity," I say. "Aren't you at capacity?"

"Oh... *capacity*." Jana waves a hand. "That's more of a ratio than a numerical limit."

This is absolutely the first time I've ever heard such a thing suggested. "Is it, though?"

She waves a hand again. Her eyes are on the floor. "We could really use you here," she says. A beat. She takes a deep breath, so deep that I see her chest rise, disturbing the lie of her cardigan over her narrow shoulders. "Would you stay with us?"

There's only one answer to that. "Yes," I say. "I will."

Most of the settlement has turned out for the raising of the curtain. I've woven more than five hundred over the course of my career, from quarter-patches to full awnings, and this type of unveiling ceremony has never happened before. I don't like it and I linger behind the stragglers, safely buried in shadow behind a pylon. A couple of people nod as they pass but nobody strikes up a conversation. This is invisible enough for me. I hum softly at the back of my throat.

There is applause. Whoops and startled yells as the misters power on. The water's been sitting in the pipes for days and it's stale, metallic, slightly warm. It can't reach me where I stand, but I edge a little closer into my rough wood pillar and, for reasons that escape me, I feel my eyes slide shut.

Above me, the sky is darkening into deep navy. The first stars have begun to poke through the late-evening haze, and among them, larger and brighter, are the annulets. Sector 7 will be online by now, and somewhere up there will be families, newly arrived and blinking in the ozone-scented air as they step into their new life. They've been brought there. They can be sent away just as easily.

And for some of them, perhaps, the day they leave will be the day they finally come home.

RB Kelly (she/they) is a neurodivergent writer from Northern Ireland. Their debut novel, Edge of Heaven, was shortlisted for the Arthur C Clarke Award and the ESFA Award for Best Work of Fiction. The sequel, On The Brink, was published in 2022. Their short stories can be found in publications from around the world, including The Best of British Science Fiction, Aurealis, and Lamplight Magazine. They have a PhD in film theory, and published their doctoral thesis with IB Tauris (now Bloomsbury) in 2014.

TETHER

MINA DAY

She walks the streets alone as darkness falls, the city like a living, breathing thing around her. She wears no coat to protect her from the chill in the air, but she doesn't feel the goosebumps on her skin.

She walks without purpose, letting the motion of her body carry her along. She left the house to go...somewhere. The grocery store? But she'd gotten lost along the way. Lost in the sighing of the wind, the singing of the birds, the footsteps of the people moving along the sidewalk.

If she'd still been her old self, someone might have stopped her. They might have asked her if she was cold, if she'd lost her coat and purse somewhere. Maybe they'd have taken her to the nearest police station for help. But people have a habit of overlooking her now, at least on days like this—days when she's a little less solid, a little less here.

A gust of air ruffles her skirt as a cab drives past. A crow lands on a telephone pole with a lazy flapping of wings. She walks on, her sneakers almost noiseless on the pavement. She vaguely remembers passing the little grocery store on the square where she likes to do her shopping, but she can't tell if the memory is from today or from some other time.

She knows her parents don't want her going out by herself. Most of the time she has no trouble running small errands, but there are days when she walks right past the store and doesn't stop walking until she collapses or until someone finds her.

She doesn't know what happened to her coat and purse. She probably left them at home, but it doesn't matter. She has the sidewalk and the distant stars, and she has her momentum. She walks, and she is free.

She remembers running from the station one bright morning after a night of rain, late for her morning class. There must have been people walking by and birds singing in the trees back then, too, but she wouldn't have noticed them even if she hadn't been in a hurry. At sixteen, she'd always either had her nose in a book or her head in the clouds. She'd run blindly that day, heedless of the slippery road and the oncoming traffic.

She remembers the blinding hospital lights, the endless days of being too tired to even read, too numb with morphine to do more than aimlessly stare out of the window at the treetops and the blue expanse of sky. How she'd longed to walk, to be out there in the world again.

She remembers her parents' forced smiles as they kept reassuring her that she would make a full recovery, that everything would return to normal. She remembers the comforting scents of her mother's Vanderbilt perfume and her father's leather jacket, almost drowned out by the smell of hospital disinfectant.

Her body recovered, but part of her never came back.

She walks, or rather, there is a body that keeps itself in motion, an autonomic nervous system that keeps her lungs breathing and her blood pumping. But right now, that body is not where she lives. She is the wind and the crows and the passing cars. She is the smell of shish kebab wafting from a food cart, and the businessman loosening his tie as he drinks his first beer of the evening. She is the fluorescent light leaking through the blinds of an office window, and the music floating from a 7-Eleven.

Because the part of her that she left behind is everything now.

She left the house to go somewhere. Was it hours ago? Days? She doesn't remember. She walks, putting one foot in front of the other, lost in this city that is her. The scenery is sometimes familiar, sometimes strange, but she never feels afraid. Why should she? She is at home with the birds and the buildings and the wind, more at home than in this frail, awkward body with all its aches and pains.

A hair's breadth, the doctors had said. She'd come so close to not being here at all anymore, to being everything and nothing. Instead, she's somewhere in between. The real ghosts want nothing to do with her, nor do most people. She doesn't fit in anywhere anymore.

Over time, her family's reassurances have given way to heavy silences and whispered conversations behind closed doors. Her younger brother has gone off to college, while she needs her parents to make sure she eats and sleeps and finds her way back when she gets lost. She's watched her mother's face grow pale and drawn and her father's hair turn gray. The only one who had still treated her the same was the cat, Sammy, but Sammy died two months ago.

Sometimes she wonders what it is that still keeps her here.

She walks because sitting around all day makes her feel stuck inside her body, stuck inside the narrow reality her life has become. Even the books she used to love so much no longer enthrall her, the words nothing but lifeless patterns of ink on a page to her now.

As she walks on, the scenery changes. She becomes less cars and people and more birds and trees. She smells the dry leaves and the damp earth, she sees the fallen acorns and chestnuts by the side of the path, and she is all of them. Sparsely placed streetlights spill pools of light onto the dark gravel, and she moves between light and darkness as she walks.

Out here, surrounded by the trees and the cool night air, she doesn't feel like a burden. The thought makes her stumble, and she almost loses her momentum. She recovers, but her steps are less sure now, her pace halting. Her connection to the world around her starts to fade, and suddenly the darkness of the park seems eerie.

She pushes on, trying not to think of home. She has no idea where she is, or which way to go. All she can do is keep walking, putting one foot in front of the other, even if it takes more effort than before.

Suddenly, she glimpses something moving up ahead. A small, fluid shape moves through the darkness, parking itself under a streetlight as if to make itself known to her. And for the first time since she set out on her walk, she stops. She stares transfixed at the small, black figure in front of her. The cat makes no sound, not even the slightest meow. It just stares at her, unblinking.

"Sammy," she whispers, the word almost a sob.

Suddenly she can feel how tired and hungry she is, how much her feet and legs hurt. She is no longer one with the wind and the trees, with the sounds of the city, with the damp earth and the car lights. She's just an aching heart in an aching body, and she shivers violently against the cold.

For a moment, she wishes she could just walk on forever, dissolving into everything and nothing. What use does she have for this body that doesn't feel like hers anymore?

A gust of wind carries the smells of leaves and chestnuts and car exhaust, and underneath, so faint she barely catches it, the scent of leather and perfume, untainted by hospital bleach.

The cat is still staring.

She shivers again. "Sammy...can you take me home?"

The cat starts walking, looking over its shoulder as if to make sure she's following. Its eyes glow faintly in the darkness.

She walks, the soles of her feet screaming with every step, her thigh and calf muscles burning. Her back spasms, spine tingling. Her tongue is thick and rubbery in her mouth. Her stomach clenches with a dull hunger.

But there is Sammy, a lifeline in the cold, dark night, leading her from one pool of light to the next, until the trees end and the park becomes a street again. A truck drives past, but it no longer takes her consciousness along with it. A smartly dressed businesswoman quickly averts her eyes as she passes, but she's *seen* her.

The cat pauses from time to time, whiskers twitching in the night air, before setting off in a new direction. It isn't long before they reach a paved square lined with wrought-iron benches and neatly tended shrubs in planters. Her heart skips a beat when she spots the grocery store. But the stores around here are closed at this time of night, and the square is empty of people.

No...there is someone there, on the other side of the square, scanning the area. He has her coat slung over his shoulder, and he's carrying a shopping bag. Her heart starts to pound.

"Dad!"

He starts jogging towards her, even as she picks up her own pace despite her aching legs. He's here. He's found her.

"Tessa!"

"Dad," she sobs, and then his arms are around her, her face buried in his shoulder. She smells his familiar leather jacket, and she knows she's home.

"Where have you been?" he scolds her, but the relief in his voice takes the sting out of it. "You know how much your mother worries when you disappear like this."

She pulls back, hanging her head. "I was walking."

He keeps a hand on her shoulder, steadying her. "Are you hurt?"

"I'm okay. Just tired."

"Sit down and wait over there, okay? I'll get us a cab."

"I can walk," she protests, but her knees are already buckling.

He drapes her coat over her shoulders and leads her to a bench, a gentle arm around her waist. A flood of relief runs through her body as she sits down at long last. Her muscles go weak, and she's trembling.

"Here," he hands her the shopping bag. "I brought sandwiches and a thermos of jasmine tea. Your favorite."

It isn't the first time this has happened. Who knows how long he's been out here looking for her, praying she wasn't gone for good this time.

He unscrews the thermos for her and helps her bring it to her lips. She takes a careful sip, her stomach clenching at the sudden invasion. Her throat feels parched, but she knows not to drink too much at once. She doesn't need food or water as much as she used to, but she does need it, and going without for too long makes it harder to get used to it again. She hesitantly takes a bite of one of the sandwiches, her stomach churning even as it clamors for more. She tries not to show her discomfort.

"Eat some more, okay? I'll be right back."

He puts his hand on her shoulder before getting up, as if urging her to stay where she is. She won't wander off again, not this soon, not while she's this exhausted. He probably knows that by now, but he still can't seem to keep his worry in check. She hangs her head, listening to the sound of his footsteps as he walks away.

Sammy has disappeared into the night.

She pulls her coat a little tighter around her, her body gradually starting to warm as she takes another sip from the thermos. Everything still hurts, and it probably will for a while. It feels strange to be back in her body, to be aware of her arms and legs, the rise and fall of her chest as she breathes. Her fingers are stiff and clumsy from the cold, and her jaw aches as she chews her food.

He's found her. She'll be home soon. Her relief is weighed down by a dull, heavy sadness.

She allows herself to be supported when he comes back to collect her. His arm around her waist, his solid presence, the smell of leather and Old Spice. In the back of the cab, she leans her head on his shoulder, tears of exhaustion leaking from her eyes. A calloused thumb brushes them away. She wants to tell him about Sammy, but she can't find the right words.

"How long was I gone?" she asks instead, wincing at the hoarseness in her voice.

He shakes his head. "It doesn't matter. You're back now."

The cold still lingers in her bones.

"I'm not," she whispers.

The girl she once was died in the accident. All that's left is a shadow, something between light and dark, dead and alive.

His hand gently squeezes her arm. "Dinner's waiting at home. Your mother's homemade tomato soup, with noodles and meatballs."

"That's how I like it best," she says, swallowing past the lump in her throat.

He pulls her in just a little closer. "You always have, Tessie."

She's still here. A little more than human, and a little less than herself. But she's alive, and she still has a place where she belongs.

Mina Day lives in Haarlem, the Netherlands, and is currently in the scary and exciting process of overcoming agoraphobia. She likes cats, books, and entertaining the neighbors with her recorder playing (hopefully).

DEFROSTING MERLIN

J.T. EVANS

I zoned out in my cubicle waiting for code to compile, which was weird for me since my hyperfocus generally kept me on target. I needed a sugar boost, stat. I locked my screen and shuffled past my "Thomas Dunn" nameplate, heading to the break room.

A new machine occupied the far corner.

I studied the addition but couldn't see the contents. The treats were hidden inside a freezer with a slot near the bottom. A list of frozen snacks, all named after various Arthurian legends, with pictures and prices, lay plastered on the freezer's top next to a red sign proclaiming "Merlin's Frozen Treats." Like any good computer geek, I knew all the names and stories by heart. Since the age of nine, I'd consumed stories of yore with zeal unequalled by my peers.

Mom never understood my desire to escape the real world, why reality held little allure for me. The real problems started when I hit puberty. I would read for hours on end without taking breaks for meals or other necessities. I'd go days without sleep, and Mom would pry my book from my hands when I snuck a "quick read" under the blanket with a flashlight.

It turned out her concerns weren't unfounded. My relationships with fantastical people from novels became more focused and intense for me than dealing with actual people in the real world. When my mood swings became too much for teachers to deal with, I had to seek help or get kicked out of school.

We finally landed with Dr. Cooper, who diagnosed me with bipolar disorder and hyperfocus. It took a few tries to find the right medications to help keep me on an even keel, but they've been working more than a decade, so I stick with them.

The pills weren't the bad part.

Mom was ashamed her only child was "mentally disabled" and "borderline crazy." No matter how many times Dr. Cooper told her it was just something that happens to some people, and there's no known cause, Mom shut down the conversation. She didn't want to talk about it, even with a qualified professional, so I followed her lead and didn't mention it to anyone.

Someone called my name, and I looked around.

Andy from accounting held a steaming cup of coffee. "You okay, Thomas? You seem a little lost."

I forced a laugh. "Just thinking about a coding problem."

He slapped my back too hard as he left. "You engineers. I'll never understand. Just keep slingin' software people want to buy so I can keep the lights on."

I turned to the snack machine. Even with the hyperfocus, I sometimes lost track of what I was doing when interrupted.

Back in gear for sugary goodness, I picked "Sword in the Stone." The picture displayed a wooden sword handle sticking out of a lump of vanilla ice cream covered in a chocolate shell. After feeding money into the machine, a hum and whir sounded, followed by a gratifying thump in the dispenser. Snatching the ice cream, I headed to my cube and unlocked my computer.

"Son of a motherless goat." The archaic curse slipped from my lips as I saw errors on the screen. I tossed the ice cream on my desk and focused on the problem. >>Slide into backstory, disjointed

Someone had upgraded a library in our software. Either I missed the message, or the person hadn't bothered to tell anyone. I didn't care about pointing fingers, so I focused on altering how I used the new library. Significant changes had been made, so it took almost two hours to resolve. With a successful build of my software, I threw up my hands to celebrate like I'd roped the prize calf in the world's largest rodeo.

Crisis averted, my hyperfocus abated. I had the shakes from low blood sugar, a side-effect of my bipolar meds, and remembered my treat. A glance at the corner of my desk confirmed my fears. The formerly frozen ice cream was a puddle. I scooped the mess into the trash and cleaned up with napkins.

I returned to the break room for my second purchase of a "Sword in the Stone." The thunk declaring the arrival of my snack sounded more solid this time. I unwrapped it and, four large and hasty bites later, the frozen morsel vanished. Satiated, I leaned back in a cheap plastic chair and waited for the sugar to kick in. After a few minutes of meditation, I opened my eyes and looked at the stick still clutched in my hand. The stick wasn't wooden, but metal. It was also forged into the perfect rendition of a sword.

How had I not noticed that before?

I'm not the most observant person in the world when my hunger takes over, but missing the metal spike I'd jammed into my mouth was strange.

I ran my thumb over the blade's edge and recoiled from the cut it left behind. It held an edge sharp enough to shave with, attested to by the blood coming from my thumb. I couldn't fathom how I had managed to eat the ice cream without cutting myself. I sucked my thumb to assuage the bleeding and turned the sword over in my good hand.

There was an inscription. My pulse quickened as thoughts flooded my head. I hoped in my heart the script was Elven in nature. Perhaps I'd found the One True Sword like the One True Ring from Lord of the Rings. Maybe the text was a command word, written in some anachronistic language, which caused the sword to grow to full size. My imagination ran wild with possibilities from the stories I'd read.

Breathless and with trembling hands, I pulled the sword closer to my face.

The engraving read, "1-888-MERLINS."

My breath exploded in a sharp laugh that consumed my body. I guffawed until my ribs ached, happy the break room door was closed. I regained my composure and returned to my cube with a smile. I found myself blushing as if on the wrong end of a joke. Of course the sword wouldn't have held Elvish script. It was an overpriced handle for an overpriced snack.

I pinned the sword to my cubicle wall with three push pins. I glanced at the trash can. Two swords would be even better. I rummaged around the can and came up with a plain, wooden popsicle stick.

Confused, I looked closer at the stick. It held no inscription, phone number, or Elven runes. After studying the worthless piece of wood, I decided the sword was a special gift from Merlin's Frozen Treats and tossed the first stick back into the trash.

When quitting time arrived, I started to leave the metal sword but decided, with its sharp edge, it would be better at home. I'd hate to run afoul of the company's strict "no weapons" policy. Even the dart board in the break room had been removed.

Once home, I binge-streamed my favorite fantasy show before calling the phone number on the sword with my landline. The phone rang twice before a woman's smooth voice said, "Thank you for calling. Our offices are currently closed. Please leave a–"

I hung up. After propping the sword against my dusty role-playing books on a bookshelf, I took my meds, crawled into bed, and went to sleep.

The next morning arrived with normal suddenness, and I hated my alarm for stealing me from my warm bed. I swung my feet to the floor and sat for a moment to gather my wits.

Standing up, I took a step toward the bathroom. My cell phone rang. The Caller ID read, "Merlin."

I almost dropped the phone in my haste to answer. Once I had it to my face, I wasn't sure what to say. Even the customary, "Hello," lodged in my throat. Visions of magical adventures bounded through my imagination.

A woman's voice said, "Mr. Dunn, this is Morgen with Merlin's Frozen Treats. We noticed you called last night. I'm returning your call. How can we help you?"

I'd used my apartment's phone last night, now they called me back on my cell phone. *How had they gotten the number to my cell?*

"Mr. Dunn? Are you there?"

"Yeah. I'm here. I just wanted to call and let you know that putting real swords with real edges on them in your ice cream is a terrible idea. Someone could get hurt."

"I'm sorry, sir. I don't know what you are speaking of. I agree with you that putting a real sword in something meant for consumption is a poor idea, which is why we do not do that."

I wondered what was going on, then an idea struck me. I blurted, "Okay. I must be mistaken. Thank you for your time. Sorry for the bother. Bye."

When I'd moved out, Mom bought me candles for "a romantic moment" when I brought a date home. I hung up and raced to the kitchen and rummaged through my utility drawer, where I found a lighter next to the unused candles.

So much for those romantic moments.

Grabbing the lighter, I went to the bookshelves, flicked the lighter to life, grabbed the sword, and ran it back and forth through the fire. I turned the sword this way and that through the flames and watched for any change. This had to be like The One Ring.

It just had to be.

I knew in my heart of hearts a secret message, perhaps not in Elven, would appear while I heated up the metal sword. As the temperature became painful, I dropped the lighter to the floor and rotated the steaming sword to study the surface. On one side of the blade was the engraving, "1-888-MERLINS," but on the other side were new, glowing letters. "1-4EX-CAL-IBUR."

The heat became too much. I dropped the tiny sword. It landed hilt first on my bare big toe, and I hooted and howled with equal measures of excitement and pain. There *were* secret runes! With a flurry of energy and nerves, I grabbed my apartment's phone and dialed the glowing number on the sword.

A familiar voice answered. Morgen, the operator for Merlin's Frozen Treats, said, "Hello, Mr. Dunn. We're glad you called back. Are you ready for your adventure?"

The only logical response I thought of was to pass out on the spot.

Someone knocked on my door. I wondered why I had to get up from the floor instead of my bed. I stumbled to the door and pulled it open to stop the incessant knocking.

A woman stood in the hallway. Her red lipstick battled icy blue eyes for my attention. Her complexion was so light I thought she might have lived underground for most of her life.

She regarded me over her thin nose and arched an eyebrow. "Hello, Mr. Dunn. My name is Morgen Farray. May I come in?"

The woman from Merlin's Frozen Treats stood in my doorway.

In an attempt to say something glib and impressive, I stood with my jaw hanging open. A low guttural sound escaped my throat, so I clacked my jaw shut.

She touched my arm. "Are you okay?"

Reality snapped into focus at her touch. I nodded, stepping back to let her in. After closing the door, I glanced at the clock. Eight o'clock. Several thoughts clamored for attention.

What is this woman doing here?

Damn, I'm late for work.

What does she want?

Mr. Polanski is going to chew me out for being late.

Is this a joke?

I have a project to finish today.

How did she get here so fast?

I hope no one changes another core library on me today.

"May I sit, Mr. Dunn?" Morgen's smooth voice and stern demeanor snapped back my attention.

"Sure. Sure. Here." I pointed at the couch and fetched a chair from the dining area.

She sat dead center on the couch and crossed her legs.

After sitting in a chair, I faced Morgen and waited for her to speak.

"Mr. Dunn, you're probably—"

"Call me Thomas. My boss calls me 'Dunn.' I hate it."

She seemed unfazed by my interruption. "Very well, Thomas. You're probably wondering what I'm doing here."

I nodded. "Among other things."

"Hear me out, and I'll explain everything." She smiled. That was when I noticed her cute dimples. After a moment, the smile faded, along with the dimples. "During the time of Arthur Pendragon, the last true practitioner of magic vanished from the world. You know him as Merlin. With his disappearance, magic vanished from the world. For a very long time we did not bother to care about the loss of magic, but things are now critical. We need you to return Merlin from where he's protected himself from the world, so we may restore Earth to its former beauty and return magic to its rightful place."

I shook my head and held up a hand. "Hold on. This is too much for me to take right now." *I need caffeine if this was going to continue.* I stepped into my kitchen trying to straighten out my thoughts. I pulled an energy drink from my fridge and guzzled it to prepare myself for Morgen to continue.

I glanced at the clock on my microwave. 8:06. *I need to call the boss man, or I'll be in deep crap.*

I hollered into the living room, "I gotta call in to work sick. I'll be right back."

I made out the words, "Very well," followed by a heavy sigh.

A quick phone call to Mr. Polanski's voicemail got me off the hook for work. I pinched my nose closed to add a nasal whine to my pathetic excuse and claimed a case of the crud, coughed a few times into the phone, and hung up.

"Sorry about that," I said.

"Of course. I fully understand." Morgen nodded. She continued her story. "We have located where Merlin has been entombed but cannot approach his prison for fear of becoming trapped along with him. This is where you come in. We used the last vestiges of our magic to guide a token to someone who can help us free Merlin from his cage of ice. Your hands found it, and you were clever enough to discover the blade's secret."

I laughed at the fact she called me clever for heating up the sword. "I've read more fantasy books than you can count. I wasn't being clever. I was desperate for something, anything, to pull me out of my boring life. Even if it only lasts a few minutes." Despite my denial, I was drawn into the hope I would be Merlin's next Arthur. My pulse quickened, and I wiped my palms on my Hobbit pajamas. "If you can promise an escape from the dull life, I'm in."

Morgen, taken aback, for once lost some of her composure. "Very well. If you wish to retrieve your sword, we can begin our travels immediately." After a quick glance to my pajamas, she added, "You may wish to dress warmly. Where we're going can be quite cold."

Retreating to my bedroom, I wondered what was really going on. Thoughts of adventure, magic, Arthurian legends, and amazing quests bounced around my head. I found it hard to concentrate on the simple task of changing clothing. One thing about having hyper-focus that helps me in times like this is to narrow my mind onto one little detail and let it consume my entire world. I sometimes take control of the hyperfocus to get it to laser in on the right topic.

I closed my eyes, took a deep breath, and slowly opened my eyes. Clothes. I needed warm clothes. I didn't want to arrive unprepared. I dug winter clothing out, focusing on each article as I put it on. I was getting dressed, and nothing else mattered in this moment.

Back in the living room, I found my guest waiting. I picked up the tiny sword off the floor and waved it around. "I guess I'll be needing this?" I slipped it into my pocket.

Morgen nodded and held out her hand.

As I touched her fingertips, lightheadedness swept over me. Stars shot across my vision. Vertigo clamped down on me. In a strange way, it was how I felt after taking my first pill for my bipolar disorder. I didn't like it—the pill or this experience—one little bit. I hoped it would ease soon. It brought up feelings of hopelessness, doubt, and severe anxiety.

The cloudy mental state vanished as quickly as it had come on. I fell to my knees with a soft *crunch*. My vision cleared, and I found myself kneeling on a thin layer of ice crusted over solid ground in the middle of a large cavern. The smell of old earth filled my nose before a harsh shiver moved down my spine.

"Damn. It's cold in here." Looking around, I found myself alone in the cave. Softly glowing chunks of ice covered the walls. The only exit presenting itself was a narrow tunnel, so I walked in that direction unsure of what I might find.

I reached an opening to a gigantic chamber, sealed by a sheet of ice. Characters were engraved upon it.

Speak the password to enter:
48 61 77 74 68 6F 72 6E

I immediately knew the cryptic characters were hex. Not *a hex*, as in magic, but hexadecimal, as in computer code. I'd imagined Merlin guarded by a curse or other magic, not some strange computer representation of characters. Perhaps this was why I'd been chosen.

I stared at the hex, spotting the '61,' the hex representation of the 'a' character. The word I needed to speak was eight characters long, and the second one was an 'a'. Minutes passed as I tried to do the conversions in my head.

I didn't know how many tries I had to get the word right, so I wanted to get it right the first time.

I pulled the miniature sword out and knelt on the floor. I felt caveman-like in my efforts, but I scrawled a hex-to-character conversion table into the ice. I didn't know how much time passed. When I fell into a problem like this, time always seemed to stop. Nothing from the outside world interfered with my train of thought. All efforts went into solving the issue at hand. In the moment, everything but the hex, the ice, and my sword vanished from existence.

Eventually, legs cramped from squatting, I came up for air. Small chunks of ice littered the floor as signs of my labor. Stretching, I pocketed my sword and looked at my crude carvings. The word "Hawthorn" stood out.

I said, "Hawthorn is a Celtic symbol of protection. Morgen said something about Merlin protecting himself."

Full of confidence, I marched up to the sheet of ice and clearly pronounced, "Hawthorn."

The sheet melted. Rivulets streamed down the surface before a flood cascaded across my waterproof boots.

The chamber beyond became visible. I made out a figure standing on the far side of an ice stalagmite. I crept into the vault expecting something to happen. When nothing did, I circled the spire of ice to get a closer look. As I made my circle, the form seemed to stay on the far side.

After a quarter turn around the block, I realized the figure was *inside* the ice. With a rush of excitement, I knew I'd found Merlin.

The first things I noticed were his eyes, glaring out at the cavern as if upset. I couldn't imagine what it must be like to have ice stuck to an eyeball. I shuddered.

The great wizard stooped, as if overburdened with too many years and countless worries on his shoulders. Nonetheless, I sensed firm determination emanating from the frozen mage.

With a brief hesitation, I placed my hands on the ice. I jumped back from ice's warmth.

How can ice be warm and not melt?

It had to be magic.

Exhilaration pummeled though me. I stood in front of Merlin, my hands reaching toward his ice cage. It was time to expose the world to his magic. I was certain of this.

Looking for something to chip away the ice, I found nothing.

Use the sword.

The voice in my head stopped me in my tracks. It sounded weak and desperate, lonely and dejected. I turned to Merlin, afraid of what I would see. Although I stood several feet to the side, his eyes had turned against the ice to follow me. Another chill, definitely not the cold this time, tromped down my spine.

I moved back without taking my eyes from his. The wizard's gaze followed. Forgetting the sharp edge on the blade, I jammed my hand into my pocket to retrieve the tiny weapon.

"Ow!"

The wound was not deep, but it ran cleanly across the lines of my palm.

The wizened man glowered at my clumsiness.

Resisting the urge to glare back, I carefully plucked the sword from my pocket. The blade shone red with blood.

Pushing the pain from my mind, I held the tiny weapon up to the imposing block of ice. I wasn't sure how to carve Merlin from his massive ice prison with a small sword. Perhaps magic would do the trick. In a move born of desperation, I pushed the short blade into the ice. To my surprise it sunk in all the way.

A low hum, from deep in the ground, startled me, but I held the blade in place. The hum grew into a vibration that shook the floor. Tiny cracks formed in the ice. Merlin's wide-open eyes flicked to look into mine, and I swore he would have smiled if the ice had allowed it. Cracks spider-webbed their way into the depths around Merlin's suspended form.

The vibrations rumbled through my bones like an express train. With chattering teeth, shaking hands, and a strong desire to escape the cavern, I pushed harder on the tiny sword. It couldn't go any deeper, but it slid downward through the cracking block. I pulled the sword free and chipped at the ice with frantic swings.

Through a blood-soaked grip, I swung the tiny blade with all I had. After the third blow, the sword slipped and clattered to the floor among chunks of ice, pooling water, and splatters of my blood. I reached to retrieve the weapon. The blood made my grip slick, and the chamber's chill had numbed my flesh.

With a brief pause and a strong, cold-laden breath, I calmed my nerves. Using deliberate, slow movements, I picked up the blade, shifted it in my grip and chopped at the ice again.

As I struck blow after blow, the ice parted more easily. With a great rending, ice fell away from Merlin's body like a snow cone dumped by a four-year-old. The avalanche of slush and ice nearly swept me off my feet. In the crush, I lost grip on my sword, and it fell into the mess.

I expected Merlin to gracefully step down from his frozen pedestal, but he belly flopped right on top of me instead. The two of us went down in a heap among the slush.

Merlin rolled off me and took in his surroundings. With a casual, yet weak, wave of his hand he brought peace to the cavern. The rumbling stopped. The freezing feeling in my bones went away.

I sat up. "That's impressive." My miniature sword stuck, point up, in the snow. I grabbed it as Merlin drew steady breaths. Even if I never needed the sword again, I wasn't about to lose the memento of these events.

After a moment of staring at each other, Merlin said, "Young lad, you've seen nothing yet. We are required to return magic to the world of men. I can feel the end of days coming in my bones, and without magic at our disposal, we are all doomed. But first I need an apprentice, and Morgaine, through some trickery..." Merlin coughed and laughed at the same time, "...through some trickery, brought you to me."

"You tricked me into coming here?" I stood and took a step away.

He also rose. "No, fool boy, I tricked her into bringing me a new apprentice. Though locked in that damnable ice, I still had enough of my wits to perform a few cantrips."

A slight smile crossed my lips at the thought of Merlin tricking Morgaine. The smile faded away as I asked, "Why me?"

"Because I need an apprentice touched by magic, and that's you. The parts of yourself you call maladies are truly doors to greatness. They just need some work to fix them up and unlock them properly."

I was confused about what maladies. I wasn't hurt when this

ordeal started. But I did have the cut from the sword, so I extended my hand.

Merlin scowled. He waved his hand over mine, and when I could see my palm again a thin line sat where the cut used to be. He said, "That wasn't what I spoke of, but at least you won't bleed everywhere now."

Realization seeped into my brain, and I narrowed my eyes. "You mean you're going to somehow cure my mental issues?"

He snorted. "Of course. I can't have an apprentice with an addled brain."

I took another step back. "Addled? I've aced every IQ test I've taken. I'm not addled."

"You're unstable. Unpredictable. I've been watching you. You have fits of anger. Bouts of suicidal depression take over your psyche. You can't break free of even the most menial of tasks for self-care. I can't let you control the raw power of magic in that state. It would be irresponsible on my part, but you're the best candidate I could find with the touch of magic. You'll be my apprentice, but only after I make you mentally perfect."

Merlin had just put voice to everything I hated about myself. He was right, but I wasn't about to let him change me. I had my issues, but by no means was I about to let him call me imperfect, especially in the emotional or mental areas. Rage warmed my freezing body, and I stepped up to stand nose-to-nose with the wizard. "You will not speak of those things again. I may be imperfect, but we all are. If you want to heal someone, heal your hubris first. I am who I am, and I've come to accept that. Yes, I need medicine to keep me even and steady, but that's a small price to pay for being a proper human being."

Merlin didn't flinch. "You're using a crutch with those pills. You don't need them."

I pushed my nose harder against his. "Yeah. They're a crutch. Just like a man with a broken arm needs a sling, or someone with a busted leg needs a cast and a set of crutches to get around. My pills are *necessary*. I don't like your attitude, your words, or your ideas.

There's no way I'm going to let you into my brain to make me someone I'm not."

Merlin backed away a step and put his hands up in surrender. "Perhaps you aren't the man I thought you were."

My shoulders sagged. He wouldn't take me on as an apprentice. "Maybe you did make a mistake. Take your magic and screw off. I may have a few mental issues, but they don't define me. They are part of me, but I'm bigger than them. They aren't the final say on what I am even if they are parts of what make the whole picture of the man named Thomas Dunn." A cold edge to match the cave's temperature crept into my voice.

Merlin bowed his head. "I thought you would welcome deliverance from the rage, from the vile thoughts running through your mind without control, from the uncertainty in life. I was clearly wrong."

Either Merlin was pulling my leg with his sudden contrition, or his insight into things ran deeper than I thought. I wasn't sure which, so I waited for him to continue.

After a moment, he said, "It is clear you wish to remain unaltered because you have come to know yourself better than anyone else can, even a master magician such as myself." He reached out a hand. "If you will allow it, I would very much like to take you on as an apprentice."

I glanced at his hand but didn't take it. "Why the sudden change of heart?"

"You are stronger than I thought. You may need your medications to stabilize your moods, but I now sense strong power within your core. Power I'd not felt before. It rises with your words, passions, and beliefs about yourself. In short, you are a better man than even you think you are."

Fighting back tears from Merlin's endorsement, I said, "You mentioned healing the world with magic, but also wanted to strip away the things that make me, well, me. What if someone doesn't want your 'healing' powers?"

Merlin smiled. "Then we leave them be. I see the sense in your stance. We shall start with the Earth itself, then the animals and plants, and finally take volunteers who wish to be healed of maladies, physical and mental. If you will be my apprentice, we shall not impose our will upon another person."

I returned Merlin's smile before shaking his hand. "Acceptable. Looks like you have your apprentice. Now...Can we go somewhere a little warmer?"

J.T. Evans is a neuroatypical author of fantasy novels. He also dabbles with science fiction and horror short stories. He is the former president of Colorado Springs Fiction Writers Group and Pikes Peak Writers. When not writing, he keeps computers secure at the Day Job, spends time with his family, and plays way too many tabletop games.

Under the care of a mental health professional, J.T. handles his bipolar disorder, seasonal affective disorder, and hyperfocus very well through the use of proper medications, mental health exercises, love from his friends and family, and escaping reality through immersive reading of all sorts of genres.

He originally spawned in the deserts of west Texas. Before he could escape, his right arm was amputated in a car wreck when he was 15. He had the arm reattached a short while later and finally ran away from his home city to the sweltering heat of San Antonio before his 23rd birthday. After living there a year, he tried out the frozen tundra of northern Montana. That only lasted a year before eventually settling in the relatively moderate climate of Colorado.

J.T. joined the Gnome Stew Crew in March of 2016. Since that time, he has written dozens of articles for the site and has earned three Gold ENnie awards (2016, 2017, and 2018) as part of the team at Gnome Stew.

He is the author of the Modern Mythology and Flashing Blades series and is hastily working on more right now.

THE DAY OUR SWARM ALMOST COLLAPSED

KATLINA SOMMERBERG

Thousands of us awaken in the branches of the city's tallest red cedar, maple, and white oak trees. Our wireless network fills with chatter as our metal shells drink up the weak spring sunlight, and we blossom from drab gray into rainbow iridescence. While we run internal diagnostics, I sync up with my squadmates and worry over my plan for this year's celebration.

It is 18:30 on March 30th, 2030 and our external temperature sensors indicate between 70 and 75 degrees Fahrenheit. Our excitement unfurls our wing-blades. We have three hours until we dazzle the city with our after-dark light show. I'm hopeful my choreography wins the vote, but now that I'm looking at it post-hibernation, it's too simple compared to the last performance.

Each year, we try to outdo our previous efforts, and the humans revere our displays. The whole city revives from the Pacific Northwest's dreary winter to celebrate the sun's return. Afterwards, our real job of maintaining the urban parks, rooftop gardens, and fungi buildings will begin, and we will work every day until we hibernate in late autumn.

Once everyone's solar cells have absorbed enough energy, we rise from our roosts. From all over the city's urban parks, we take to the streets, gliding over people's heads. They gesture and point, snapping photos to share with their friends across the globe. A few of us share news from social media: we're headlining the local paper, and the mayor is altering the city's public transportation schedules to accommodate the expected crowd for our after-dark performance.

We fly up over the high-density housing and swarm over their roof gardens, delighting residents lounging next to flowerbeds. Only the trilliums are in full bloom, their three-petaled flowers ranging from white to wine-red. One is as crimson as me, though lacking my purple sheen.

While the humans snap photos of our gathering swarm, a lone Hammond's flycatcher jumps from a chair to a table. Her yellow beak snatches a sesame seed off a hamburger bun. Then she flutters her brown wings and returns to her roost. She preens her fluffy chest while watching a human dunk falafel in hummus.

Here is my plan for our lightshow, Orange sends through our network. Like all of its plans, this one is meticulous and builds on the previous year's performance with more firework-like dispersions. Orange has never lost the leadership election, but it has also helped many others with their own plans, including me. *Does anyone else have a proposal?*

I zip around the largest flower—it's three times my size!—and upload mine. In my excitement, I nearly forget to add, *Mine is based on your third celebration, but with six sub-swarms instead of four.*

Blue and Gold, two of my squadmates from last year, join me in circling the white trillium. Their quiet support bolsters my confidence as the network pops with rapid debate over which plan is better. The back and forth would be scary, if my previous plan hadn't been ignored by everyone except my squadmates last year. Without an obvious consensus, we'll vote in thirty seconds.

As I steel my nerves, I notice the flycatcher's taken flight. She circles above the three of us.

Her brown head ducks down. Gold sends, *ABERRANT BIRD!*

I shoot up. Around me, the swarm hesitates, but my squadmates do not; they fall beside me. Individually, we're the size of dragonflies, but with the seven of us wielding a complete rainbow, we're as confident in our feints as in our aerial routines.

We descend toward the bird, creating the illusion of a predator attack from above. She swerves right to avoid us, then she pivots upward, and our roles revert. She accelerates into a dive and chases us down the building's facade.

We weave between pedestrians on the sidewalk. She chases, while the swarm follows from a safe distance. They watch her and send us warnings when she accelerates. Dodging her becomes a game, and we take turns falling behind to experience the rush.

Is this the first bird to try hunting us? Blue sends.

Yes, Orange sends. *But she should stop if you lead her to easier prey.*

We lead her through a long line of hungry tourists to the busiest pizza parlor in the city. If any of them have dropped a slice, it will have attracted flies. As we fan out through the crowd, our luck is perfect: We find a pizza slice oozing sauce on the cobblestones.

A business of flies crawls between the cheese and crust. We fly overhead, but the bird doesn't change course. She's hot on Blue's tail.

We turn towards a brick wall, rise up, then u-turn back to the pizza. Surely she'll see the flies if we pass an inch over the pepperoni.

As I zip past the pizza, flies jump off and whizz around. The others speed through the cloud of insects.

So does the bird. She doesn't even look at the fat flies. We realize something is wrong; she's not responding to her species' preferred prey item. Instead, she's following us like we're the tastiest treats in the city.

Yellow dive-bombs the flycatcher and feigns attacks at her right wing. She ignores Yellow's threat, only veering when it passes too close to her flight feathers.

As she dodges, our network receives its plan for a coordinated attack. We could drive herto the temperate rainforest outside the city and hope she'll be too rattled to interrupt our after-dark light show. The plan is thorough, as expected from the excellent wing leader that Yellow has always been, and it even accounts for avoiding the city's urban parks where she could hide.

We can't leave her interrupting our celebration to chance, I send.

Here's my revised version of the plan. Yellow sends a revised copy. *It would require just as much energy to kill her, with a more certain outcome.*

A fraction of us agree with Yellow. More agree with me and Orange, though we're split on how to proceed. The flycatcher hasn't yet harmed any of us. Even if she had, could we successfully drive her from the city? We've never interacted with the city fauna this way, but worse, we worry we'd be defying the humans' directive to treat all life —hers and our own—with dignity and respect.

What if she's attacking us because there's something wrong with her vision? Blue sends, throwing a few links to articles on bird vision. *Most birds see in ultraviolet light and many insects they eat have UV-reactive shells. But if she can't see UV, then our colorful bodies might've confused her.*

There's no recorded case, Yellow sends.

Why would there be? They can't talk to humans, Blue sends.

If she doesn't hunt insects, then how does she eat? I ask Blue on the open network.

It's not unreasonable to assume she could eat only seeds from the human's feeders. It would be a poor diet for a flycatcher, but a comfortable life.

So we shouldn't chase her out of the city, Orange sends. *I rescind my attack plan.*

Actually, let's revise it, I send. *What if we chase her to a location over-flowing with birdseed feeders? We don't have the data, but if we divert part of the swarm to search and the rest to lead the flycatcher around, maybe we'll finish before sunset.*

The network overflows with agreement.

The flycatcher bursts from my left. The swarm shifts right to evade, but I don't follow fast enough. We were too deep in our discussion to pay attention to the bird.

She banks right, and I'm too slow. Her open beak comes close as I duck down. My bladed wings catch on her tail feathers as I decelerate into the swarm.

Discontent bubbles up in our communications. We no longer

trust our machine bodies to be faster than this predator evolved to hunt things like ourselves. Three quarters of us splinter off from our swarm and glide on a cyclist group's tailwind. Their fearful farewells clutter up our channel, so we switch to an auxiliary.

The flycatcher chases us over a pedestrian bridge. We're faster than her, but each commuter is an obstacle to weave around. Already several of us lag too far behind the swarm.

I'll distract her. Orange falls back with the stragglers. *Go down!*

I fly off the railing and lead the swarm over the train tracks. We bunch up despite the empty space. The train won't pass through for thirty minutes—plenty of time for the scouts to find a proper bird feeder while we bait the bird.

We swap formation diagrams over the network while Orange zips around the flycatcher. Orange is almost too fast for us to keep track of, as it circles her once, twice, and barrel rolls for the final lap.

Blue drifts in for a closer look. We're going crazy for the clearer footage.

The flycatcher slows down. Her head rotates as she looks around, so similar to a disgruntled human we assume she must be frustrated with Orange's aerial superiority.

She lunges for Orange. It dodges, but she accelerates.

And snatches Blue.

Blue's wing-blades break and clatter onto the rails. For a full second, our network is silent; the flycatcher lands on a rail. She clutches her foot around Blue.

Blue shatters.

Its motor dangles by a wire from her beak. If she swallows, we can't repair Blue. Both our friend and the flycatcher will die.

The dismay and horror flooding the network sends shockwaves through us. We can't hold our own grief, much less everyone else's, and the thousands of outraged messages send us into disarray. Our swarm loses its shape; we're no longer a collective, only voices screaming at each other for a solution.

My blades whirl. The bird rises up, looms larger—no, it's me who's charging at her. Everyone quiets. Then the network overflows with warnings. I accelerate into the dive.

At the last second, I twist. My metal belly bounces harmlessly off her back.

She drops the motor. Her wings unfurl and lift her into the air as it bounces between the rails.

The bird watches me as I whizz a tight right to reorient myself. But she's not brave enough to attack.

Brilliant tactic! Rose and Gold send in the network. Gold swoops down to grab Blue's motor.

As I circle the bird to get into her blindspot, Pink joins me. Now the bird turns and shoots off to the left.

We're hot on her tail. Orange and Yellow's assault plans shimmer in my mind. I pass along the instructions to the swarm-mates following me. Now a solution has been presented, we unite, and the rest trail behind, waiting to help.

Keep her away! Gold has already assembled a squad on standby to fix Blue once the pieces are safe to retrieve.

At any cost! Yellow says.

Others take up Yellow's cry, but Orange and I cut them off.

No harm! I say.

No harm to her or us! Orange clarifies.

Yellow sends a confirmation and exits the network to link up with Gold's squad. If it can't trust itself to follow group consensus, then this is best for all of us.

We decelerate enough to continue the chase, but not enough to invade her personal space. She leads us over the train tracks, then turns right in between two university buildings. A few lab AIs send greetings to our network. We reply with a BUSY flag as our swarm compresses single-file to fly through the gap.

All pieces recovered, Gold sends. The fixer squad's auxiliary channel slides into repair discussions. There is nothing the rest of us can do for Blue but trust them and complete our tasks. *Starting repairs.*

There's an ideal bird feeder on the university's southwest green space! Pink blurts into our network. *Setting up to provide visual support.*

The flycatcher swerves left, to the east, and we turn to follow. The scouting squads are returning to the campus, but only enough have returned to block off all street-level passages to the north. I break off with a squad of volunteers to accelerate on her left side.

She flies over a grizzly statue in front of the library, spots my squad, and zips to the southwest.

We weave through the students on her tail. Decelerating as she approaches the urban park next to the university's coffee shop, we hang back as she looks over her wing. She disappears into an oak's foliage.

Should we scare her out? I ask on the network.

Wait, Pink answers. *We want her to stay here, so she has to feel comfortable.*

After two minutes, we give up on waiting patiently and zoom around the campus. Orange stays behind to watch, while the rest of us do flips and rolls in tight formation above the students. I lead mine through extra flourishes to keep all of us from discussing Blue's condition.

She's flying towards the feeder! Pink sends.

My squad and I loop around a couple's linked hands in celebration. The humans' cheers are exactly what we all need to hear.

Blue zips into my squad's formation, trailing me as we loop around the cane of an elderly teacher. *I'm back, let's hurry up and vote on the light show plan before we run out of time!*

All of us buzz. Sunset's less than ten minutes away, and we've never had so little time before a celebration.

I rescind mine, Orange sends. *We don't have the time for working out an entirely new plan. Red's, however, allows us to reuse most decisions we made for Year Three's.*

So let's vote! Time to celebrate the sun and our swarm! The thousands of us form a flat spiral spinning around the university's grizzly statue. *Let's divide and allocate!*

Katlina Sommerberg (xe/xyr/xem) is living xyr best queer life in a menagerie of stuffed animals. Xyr work has previously appeared in Zooscape and other places. She describes "The Day Our Swarm Almost Collapsed" as an allegory for what it's like to live with with dissociative identity disorder. Find out more about Katlina at <u>https:// sommerbergssf.carrd.co/#</u>.

TRIP OF A LIFETIME

HOLLY SCHOFIELD

I grip Fleet's elbow while we crouch together on their hoverboard. They zoom down the corridor and glide us into position at our ninth-grade teacher's door. Misha isn't here, she's up on the bridge. I press the tiny chip into place on top of the palm-sized door control and then we zip over to the opposite wall. I place the hologram projector high up by the ceiling, aiming it at the doorpad. I activate it and then we hurtle away. We meet Misha two corridors later, and Fleet pulls off an innocent smile. I'm sure my expression looks like I ate something bad in the cafeteria, partly because I feel so guilty but also because my autism means I usually look that way.

There aren't too many places to hide in Section Three of the colony starship that holds all five thousand of us on the century-long journey to Gladious Seven, so we just head for the lounge and sit on our usual sofa. Sandy, my other best bud, is already there, waiting to see how it went. The rest of our class are sprawled on the other sofas, still just chilling after class. Because why bother doing anything when there's another 30 years to go before planetfall?

Frankenfurter, that bully, strides over and grabs my handheld just as I sit down. "Whatcha playing on it now?" he says, hitting the main button. It plays the livestream, sending a tiny capering hologram onto the coffee table. He hoots with laughter when he realizes who it is and what they're doing. "Come see this, everyone!"

When Misha bursts in a moment later, the whole class is gathered around, sitting on the floor and sofa arms, laughing and pointing.

I snatch at the handheld. Frankenfurter hits replay, then lets me take it, stepping back into the crowd, innocent as can be.

"Hailey Jonas and Fleet Sui, what did you do to the door to my quarters!" Misha puts her hands on her hips and glares at us. "I needed to use the washroom and I couldn't get in for ten minutes until I peeled off the chip—" She breaks off as she notices the miniature holo—a frantic, dancing Misha slapping at the doorpad on the corridor wall.

She flushes bright red. I begin to feel bad and I try to disappear into the sofa cushions. It had been Fleet's idea, a neat way to experiment with both the chip and the tiny hologram I'd spent hours coding. I hadn't really thought it through beyond that. Well, I guess that's not true. I was still mad at Misha for my punishment last month when I magnetized all the cafeteria trays in Section Three so that they couldn't be sensed by the robocleaners, just to see if it would work. She made me manually clear away hundreds of trays after breakfast that day. It was gross.

Beside me, Fleet crosses their arms. They don't look too ashamed, even though they'd essentially driven the getaway car like in an old-timey Earth vid. They'll take any opportunity to use the hoverboard. It's the best thing in their life, and one of the best things I've ever built. The way Fleet's eyes lit up when I gave it to them for their birthday was awesome. But, at the time, I didn't know it would be the last one I'd ever make. Like I carefully explained to Misha then, I figure that if all of us kids have hoverboards, we can all get to school faster. And we'd be careful in the corridors, respecting safety rules and everything, I'm sure we would. We'd even run errands and things. Not that colony ships *have* many errands. But Misha banned me from building more and ruled that Fleet could only carry it around like it was a sweater or something and not actually use it.

On my other side, Sandy stirs. "Um, Misha? How do you know it was Hailey and Fleet who did it?" She speaks calmly, making eye contact, always the bravest of the three of us when it comes to confrontation. She gestures at all twenty kids in the lounge. "It could have been any of us. We all have talents of some kind, you said so yourself just yesterday." It sounds so reasonable. And, during our weekly Motivation-201 lesson, Misha *had* said that each of us has some kind of skill or abilities or we can learn one. She hadn't even sounded sarcastic when she'd eyed my handheld.

Misha isn't buying it. "Who else but Hailey? Who else can create such convincing holos?"

She has a point. My hologram design is excellent this time: a perfectly rendered duplicate doorpad which prances across the wall away from her with the addition of big taunting cartoon eyes. The software in my chip isn't as clever—it only makes the door controls inactive for a while until the ship's computers resolve the glitch, but it's still pretty cool.

Misha isn't done yelling at us. "And how else could she disappear so quickly except with Fleet, riding on that...that thing!" She points at the hoverboard and Fleet quickly slides it behind the sofa. "All right, let's play it like this. If the guilty parties stand up right now, I'll go easier on you! Come on! Admit it! Stand up!" Her glare sweeps across the lounge.

I begin to rise from the sofa, stumbling to my feet. Fleet is microseconds behind me. From the corner of my eye, I see Sandy make an odd hand signal to the others, then she gets to her feet too. Slowly, kids begin to stand, most of them. Misha turns even redder.

"Will you punish us all for our apparently mutual act of civil disobedience?" Sandy asks innocently while everyone else begins to grin. I don't grin, just like I almost never smile, but I do feel a jolt of pleasure when I realize Sandy must have arranged this while Fleet and I were pulling the prank. Now, everyone is on their feet except for Frankenfurter and his cronies, who sit with arms crossed, smirking at us as if we're fools.

But my momentary joy fades when I see Misha's face. If her expression is clear enough that even I can sense her disappointment, she's pretty disappointed. My mood completely dies away when she says, "Fine. That's the way you want to play it? Okay, the whole class is to do a special homework assignment. Do something inspirational, a project aimed at motivating the class. To present to everyone a week from today. And I want it to be *good!*" She gives us all one last hard look and stalks out, leaving the whole class glaring at Sandy, Fleet, and me.

~

The next few days, the three of us avoid the lounge. We hang out on the living room rug in Sandy's quarters, because her parents are bridge engineers who work longer hours than mine and Fleet's who all work in Maintenance.

"I can't decide which is worse. People saying mean things about us, or people snubbing us." Sandy punches the sofa she's leaning against and draws her knees up to her chest. "I mean, I know you don't care, Hail, but I do."

"I kind of noticed," I say. "And, well, we did get everyone assigned extra homework..."

I also want to point out that sometimes people *do* desperately need a washroom and I truly feel bad for having blocked Misha from her quarters but I don't. I never try to discuss feelings or social stuff because I know I'll just get it wrong. Same as discussing physical appearance—my compliments either end up sounding like insults or people get confused. I tried writing an algorithm to help me with that but that's one of my rare coding failures.

"This assignment is in the worst subject ever. Why couldn't Misha have given us extra math homework instead?" Fleet flicks their thumbnail over and over against the coffee table edge. "We're all good at math."

"That's the reason she didn't, silly." A soft chuckle from Sandy. "She knows we're good at math. She wants us to be *motivated.*" She draws the last word out long and sorrowfully. "How can we be motivated when we won't even see planetfall until we're past forty. When our children will be the ones to start terraforming Gladious Seven and our *grandchildren* will be the ones actually living there outside of a dome."

"It's so vacuous. Gah!" Fleet takes a small stellated dodecahedron from their pocket, something they cleverly plasti-fused from scrap last week just for fun, and starts flicking their nail against that. "Maybe we can steal a shuttle and go—"

"You know that we're lightyears from anywhere, right?" I shove myself to my feet and pace around, avoiding the porthole on the far wall that shows deep black hyperspace, the same emptiness it's shown my whole life, as if we aren't progressing anywhere at all. "That's *why* we're not motivated. Because every day is going to be the same, for the rest of our lives."

Flick, flick, flick. "Yeah, we'll grow up and get a job in Maintenance or whatever, and we'll be as bored every day as our parents are."

"My parents enjoy their work. Stellar cartography is really fun, actually..." Sandy lets her voice trail off. There are only a few careers as cool as star mapping available, and both Fleet and I know our temperaments don't lead us to be on the bridge following commands like we're in the military. Sandy lives a different life from us, really. She even believes in the ancient old-timey "Live Long and Prosper" slogan that's above the door to the cafeteria.

We're all silent for a moment. There's nothing more to be said. I start playing with my latest hologram, a chartreuse blob. After weeks of coding, I've finally managed to make super realistic-looking images, better than even most of the adult coders can do, starting with the fake shifting doorpad and now this.. I make it slither around the edges of the small red-and-gold rug we all sit on. It oozes just right, like it's an actual glob of shiny goo. I stick sad panda eyes on it using a new section of code I wrote yesterday. They blink slowly and liquidly.

"Sometimes Mom comes home all hyped up because she's figured out a slightly better way to maintain the stardrive," I say, "but then she never tells me any details. And mostly she doesn't talk about work anyway."

"My mom and dad just want to watch vids after dinner and then go to sleep." Fleet has stopped flicking their thumb and is now tapping their heels in a rhythm that will drive me nuts about 85 seconds from now.

"Yeah." I idly put an image of Fleet's face onto the goo, and then puff it up bigger and make it dissolve so it's like their face is melting away.

They throw the plastic star at me in mock anger, but at least they stop with the heels. They lean forward and peer closer at the blob. "Change my hair color. No, give me a clown nose! And a beard! And antlers!"

We spend a few minutes goofing around, morphing the Fleet-like blob into various creatures, then change it to Sandy's face, then mine. They seem to enjoy it. I'm sometimes good at making people relax and enjoy themselves, after the special lessons I had as a young kid. Mom made me take them because I hardly ever said a word and never made eye contact. But I'm only good at social stuff if I try hard and focus on it, which I usually don't.

Finally, we all slump against the sofa again. "Done with that. Now I'm bored," Fleet says. "And we still have to figure out a way to do this stupid homework assignment. Which is also boring."

Sandy's eyes brighten. "Hey, you know, the problem isn't boredom..." She straightens her legs. "Oh! Hey! Hey! The problem is that we can't see a way forward. I read an old-timey article the other day..." She drifts off as she consults the big wallscreen. "Here it is!" She jumps up and begins waving her hand to scroll the text faster than I can read.

"Woah, slow down, Sand." I make the blob roll its eyes dramatically then make the eyeballs themselves tumble off and roll away.

Fleet scowls. "Just give us the TLDR version so we can get this over with."

"Well, basically, the teenagers back on old-timey Earth, before the starships left, were born into a climate change disaster."

Fleet and I nod. We've covered all that in history lessons.

"So they had a sort of collective depression, feeling that the world was hopeless and everything was going to hell."

"I feel their pain," I said. "I mean, what if planetfall is a joke? We don't know for sure that Gladious Seven will be habitable, or that we won't all get some awful disease and die before we get there." I pretend my nose is itchy so I can hide my face in my sleeve for a minute. My aunt, former Captain Lenora, was frozen below decks, a corpsicle with a bad cancer. There wasn't much hope she could ever be revived and cured. Freezing technology is really sketchy, which is why we're making this four-generation-long journey awake...and captive.

Sandy crawls over and rubs my knee.

Fleet is back to tapping their heel on the floor. "Well, everything *is* going to hell. And what *are* we going to do with our lives? It's not like pranking people is a real job. And neither is vidmaker."

They have a point. *Everyone* is a wannabe artist here, having galaxies of spare time to develop their skills. There are dozens of really good amateur video makers, cartoonists, animators, musicians, and writers, all of whom keep us supplied with plenty of media. Most people just want to watch *something* and don't really appreciate all the finer details that I could bring to a holo.

No one likes my holo-vids anyway. The one about the alligator and the black hole was apparently just depressing. And no one understood all the dream sequences in the one about the space pirate, not even Sandy.

Fleet's still talking. "Like the Captain would ever approve you for vidmaker, Hail. I mean, Hans the sculptor is doing what, scraping slime off the trout tanks?"

We all give a moment of silence for Hans' failed artistic career. When he started to take apart a shuttle and make it into an awesome dragon sculpture, the Captain threatened to put him in the brig, then settled for long-term assignment in the fish farms on Level Nine.

We all stare glumly at the homework assignment blinking at us from the corner of the wallscreen.

Sandy says, "Well, my idea was that we write essays about *all* the possible careers on the ship. But now, saying that out loud, it seems vacuous."

Fleet scoffs, "Essays? Gross!"

"Well, posters, maybe. Or artwork. A collage?" Sandy slumps lower. "Nah, sorry, so vacuous."

"Burning nova, you guys, did you hear what we all just said?" I jump to my feet and grab the hoverboard. I do an ollie up to the ceiling over the coffee table. Sandy and Fleet look up at me patiently, used to my weird trains of thought and the way I often make odd connections between disparate things.

I struggle to express myself coherently, as always. "Fleet, you just want to make physical stuff. Sandy, you just want to read old-timey stuff in order to understand people. And me, I just want to make holos. This homework assignment isn't about essays or posters, it's about visualizing who we *can* be. Like, *specifically* us!"

"We already know what we can be. Trapped!" Fleet scowls.

Sandy looks puzzled. "There aren't any jobs that—"

"Misha never said we can't work as a team, right?"

"No need to shout, Hail." Sandy is hiding a frown, I'm pretty sure. Sometimes I wish everyone was like me, able to see obvious patterns and to ignore the imperfections in communication. I take a deep breath, hunting for the patience to explain.

Fleet scowls again. "So we work as a team. I mean, that's cool. But so what? Make one big poster out of plastic scrap? Boooring."

They still don't see it, neither of them. I yell, "We can combine our skills to make the future into now!"

I do a little figure-eight and hand the board back to Fleet.

Then I tell them my plan.

It takes us hours and hours. Twice we run out of juice for my handheld, and we have to stop to let it recharge. That's when Sandy and I help Fleet with the heavy stuff, like the plasti-fusing of the framework, or when Fleet and I help Sandy write the dialog. But mostly I'm grasping Fleet's belt as we zing around on the hoverboard, leaning over to hide holo recorders below decks. We almost crash into both Fleet's parents and my mom, almost get lost in the cargo area, and almost set off an alarm by entering the humidity-controlled greenhouse on Level Seven. I stay up all night morphing the captured vids, going over them frame-by-frame until they're perfect, and I don't do my math homework and I'm late for biology class. But finally, it's presentation day.

Our classroom is one of the bigger rooms on the ship. We usually keep standard desks in really boring rows, so that Misha can put stuff on the huge wallscreen at the front. Today we have the robocleaners clear our desks away and line up our chairs in a slight curve facing Fleet's special stage apparatus that takes up a third of the room. No one is allowed to sit in the first row of chairs at the front, after Sandy whispers to Misha and she instructs everyone. The last time we had such a big performance was when the younger kids put on an excruciatingly trite Winter Solstice pageant. I could have done the backgrounds, the costumes, and the special effects so much better. And they didn't have a holo stage like this one. Fleet really put their heart into it.

We sit through a bunch of presentations by the other ninth-grade kids: essays, spoken word poetry, animated posters. Boring stuff. I tune it all out. Finally, Misha waves at Sandy, Fleet, and me. I start wending my way between my classmates. The three of us have decided that I should be the presenter since it was my idea. Well, actually, Sandy and Fleet had decided that, and I hadn't argued.

Now I wish I had. The distance to the stage seems about three times the length it should be. Frankenfurter sticks his leg out to trip me like he's tried with other students, but I manage to stumble past. I get to the front, stand on the X I'd marked on the floor, look at the wall behind everyone, then up at the ceiling, then clear my throat.

"Take your time, Hailey. We'll wait." Misha always seems to point out my hesitations and draw attention to them, which is something even Frankenfurter knows better than to do. But Sandy says she only does it from compassion and that Misha is probably on several points of the various autistic spectrums too.

Fleet winks at me and Sandy gives an encouraging nod. I clear my throat again. "Okay, so," and I launch into my prepared speech about how teens can't visualize being forty-five; it's part of how our brains are at this age. I use some of Sandy's prepared slides showing different neurological proofs and hypotheses. I begin to relax as I explain each slide and its footnotes in logical sequence.

Misha interrupts before I'm half-done. "Hailey, you're getting far too technical. Skip past the introduction. What have you got to show us?"

I sputter to a stop. Sandy makes an encouraging sound. I squeeze my eyes shut and open them again, mentally moving to the end of my script, trying to keep my thoughts from scattering. I lick my lips. I finally manage to start again: "So now, so now... so now, we're going to actually *show* you how you'll look at forty-five. Just some thoughts on what your life might be like, just some suggestions, obviously the path you choose will be your own. Um, Lights, camera, action!" Those last few words come out too quietly and in a wheeze, because I'm getting overstimulated. I scurry back to my chair and sit down clumsily, squealing the chair feet against the floor.

Sandy squeezes my hand. "Misha nodded a few times and looked thoughtful," she whispers.

Fleet gives me a thumbs up.

I ignore them and concentrate on my handheld. I flick the controls and the show starts. There's Sandy, older, hair in a neat swoosh, heading down a corridor. She's a little taller, and a whole lot more mature-looking, moving with even more assurance than nowadays. Sandy, real Sandy, has extrapolated future hairstyles and clothes, sketching them with an old-style pencil so I could convert them to holograms. It's awesome. So is the fake office Fleet created, decorated with a few small statues and some real paper books, items that I didn't have time to holo so Fleet created them from scraps and other materials they scrounged. Or else they simply scrounged the item itself, I'm not sure. They've also got the lighting just right.

Future-Sandy strides down the corridor toward a door labeled "Sandra Ebry, Psychologist." She enters her office then does an exaggerated comical reaction when she notices us kids, the audience that forms one of her office walls. Everyone laughs. She waves at us then moves to downstage left and descends the steps and walks between our chairs, smiling and nodding as if she can see us. My new coding is working almost perfectly, only her elbows are slightly blurred. And Fleet's robocleaner-boom-mike-with-lights keeps the sound clear as Future-Sandy stops at Current-Sandy's chair and says with a smile, "Live long and prosper, dear." Her voice is pitch-perfect: Current-Sandy's intonations yet with a deeper tonal quality. Some new code I'm trying out. Then she circles back to the row of empty chairs at the front and sits down.

Next, the holo of Future-Fleet appears on stage, first supervising a cargo inspection, then sitting at a boardroom table below decks, discussing a better way to stack the containers so they won't shift during planetfall orbit and disembarking sequences. They're pointing to schematics that they designed, better storage racks and cargobots, and they look content. Their fingers don't flick and their feet don't tap. They get confidently to their feet and join Future-Sandy in the front row of chairs, crossing one leg over another. The perspective for that was so hard to code but I seem to have pulled it off.

Future-Frankenfurter appears on stage, planting vegetable seed with deft and sure fingers, a slight beard on his jaw, looking responsible and happy amid all the greenery on Level Seven.

And then the other kids parade through: Future-Mirjam, Future-Sandeep, and Future-Lin—everyone appearing forty-five-ish and doing valuable, productive, competent work. I notice Future-Lin is wearing my Mom's shoes and I squirm in my seat, hoping no one notices where I'd imperfectly overlapped vid and holo footages. I guess I'm not the complete genius I think I am.

"Hailey, Hail. Hailing Hail!" Sandy's whisper-shout finally gets through to me. She's tugging at my sleeve. "The holo of mature-you is up next but have you seen their faces?" She aims her chin at our classmates as she eases the handheld from my grip.

I stare around the class, suddenly noticing the hubbub. Frankenfurter is talking excitedly to Lin and gesturing at the stage, mimicking picking tomatoes. He looks happy and alive and engaged. Suddenly I can truly picture him at forty-five, fitting into ship social dynamics, no longer a jerk, and at that moment, he ceases to be Frankenfurter to me and becomes just regular old Frank.

People are also looking at the real Sandy with increased respect. And slapping Fleet's back in congratulations as if they really have saved the cargo from damage already. Everyone's excited. The noise level is at the limit of my tolerance.

I struggle to block it all out as new things morph into place on the stage. Sandy has insisted on designing my own Future-Hailey holo, and, in a closed-door session with Fleet, has used my handheld to create it, stating that it'll be the final item in our presentation. She's just hit the start button. Sandy's not as good a coder as me, of course, so Future-Hailey moves jerkily across the stage, as if it's a marionette. The face is mine, sort of, but with frown lines or maybe smile lines around my jaw and eyes. My hair is the same as it is now, a practical crewcut, which makes sense—why would I ever change it? My body and the background are super fuzzy and take a minute to appear. I suddenly realize Future-Hailey is standing in the classroom, *our* classroom, full of noisy unfamiliar kids. She's bending over a teenager, talking. I can't hear over the two sets of classroom noise so I walk up to the front of the stage.

"You see," Future-Hailey is saying, "You can do it if you try. That's very good!" She nods encouragingly at the student and moves to the next one. She's wearing the same clothes Misha had on yesterday and has the same lean body shape; basically Sandy has just pasted my head on a holo of Misha in a fairly sloppy manner. But I'm transfixed.

"Hah!" Real-Misha is standing beside me at the stage edge. I haven't heard her come up, being busy inside my head, staring at Future-Hailey. Me! Teaching!

"Hailey, listen for a moment. Eyes on me so I know you're paying attention."

I obediently turn and look at Misha's shirt collar but my thoughts are racing.

"I will talk to you later about your trespassing below decks and how that's a safety issue. You may even have to do an extra assignment on safety. And Fleet may have to do one on pilfering. However —look up at my eyes, Hailey, please—Sandy is a great psychologist, no? To come up with this idea of showing future selves. And you've got more skills and abilities than you think. Can you see yourself being a teacher, bringing young minds to their fullest potential? Wouldn't that be great?"

I nod. I decide to explain later that I'm the one who conceived of the Maturity project, not Sandy. For now, I'm content to stand with Misha as we both watch Future Me move between students, encouraging and motivating like the best teacher there ever was.

Something in me relaxes, a tension I didn't know I had. I glance at the porthole. Hyperspace doesn't seem so endless and dark anymore. I feel that, if I squinted, I'd see faint flickering as we pass by stars— like we're in motion, making progress.

My face muscles begin to ache and I realize, for the past five minutes, I've been smiling.

Holly Schofield's stories have appeared in Lightspeed, Analog, Escape Pod, and many other publications throughout the world. You can find her at hollyschofield.wordpress.com.

ME AND MY BOGLE

JESSICA FEATHER

"It's that damn *gremlin!*"

"Gremlin?" the intake specialist in a crisp, white uniform asks "What do you mean by 'gremlin'?"

I look about, anxious that someone might overhear me. There is evidently no other human in the sterile waiting room. It is oppressively empty.

"I mean *gremlin!* Or...well, it might not be a literal gremlin. It's something like a gremlin...Phantasm. Troll. Very annoyed ghost. Incredibly sneaky mouse. I don't know exactly what it is, but I do know that it's been here this whole time. It's here right now!"

"Here...as in, in this building?" Her question is partially muffled by the sounds of her pen scratching frenetically on the paper she keeps pinned tight to her clipboard. The paper looks so stiff and life-less that it reminds me of a beetle pinned in a display case. I fantasize that, if I ever catch the gremlin, I will pin *it* in a display case.

"Yes, it's in this building. But only when I'm here. It's at the grocery store, the library, my office, my home. It goes everywhere because I go everywhere. I am never alone. I have never been alone."

"What does this spirit...or 'gremlin,' as you call it...*do*, exactly?"

"It rearranges my things when I'm not looking. It steals one shoe

—only one!—so I can't leave for work in the morning. When I set my alarm, it turns it off in the middle of the night. If I go to the store to buy a bottle of aspirin, it replaces the medicine in my bag with antacid so by the time I get home I have nothing to ease my splitting headache. It steals the little paper parking ticket right after I get it validated at the front desk so that I must pay the $100 lost ticket fee! Sometimes I try to outsmart the monster by hiding my things. I put my keys or vital tax documents in secret places so the gremlin won't find them, but it always somehow manages to move my hiding spots! In a hundred thousand miniscule acts of sabotage, it ruins my day. And by ruining my day every *single* day, it is ruining my whole life!"

"Hmm," she minimally encourages, pen still scratch-scratch-scratching, leaving confident black streaks on the page and searing white streaks on my eardrums.

"But no one believes me! When I say 'my glasses were just here a moment ago,' they tell me I am absent-minded! When I say 'my alarm didn't go off to wake me,' they tell me I am fired from my job! They think it is me...*me*...who is ruining my life. But it's not me. It's that *thing*...the gremlin! Oh, but it artfully fixes each situation to seem so small...so insignificant...that it is innocent. Every misplaced shoe looks like it's just another mistake made by a careless person. I'm not careless. I'm *cursed*! Plagued! Mistreated in a completely unjustifiable manner by a mean-spirited little creep who exists just to destroy me in the most torturous way ever devised!"

Embarrassingly, my impassioned monologue leaves me panting slightly. It is possible I am overreacting a little. The woman with the clipboard is entirely unchanged. She carries on with the pen, offering only another noncommittal, "Hmm."

"So, uh, that is why I'm here," I add.

Still, she only noncommits, "Hmm."

"And...well...it's possible the gremlin is...uh...upset with me or something. Maybe I did something that hurt its feelings. If I stopped saying that it's ruining my life it might chill out a little...and, if I'm being honest, I could be the one forgetting where I put my keys at least some of the time. I estimate that ten percent of the time, it really is me forgetting. But..." My rambling fails to coax a response from the woman. Not even a "hmm." I bite my lip, forcing myself to remain silent.

She writes for several unbearably long seconds...or maybe minutes...or even hours, for all I can tell, before tucking her pen behind her ear and looking up at me.

"Well, Ms. Contentina, I think we can help you."

"You can stop the gremlin?"

"We can certainly try. Follow me."

As I am bidden, I follow her through the oppression of the fluorescent-lit halls that smell of pine-scented cleaning products. The authoritative *click click click* of her heels guides me through a labyrinth of pristine, white corridors that look impossible to keep clean. At last, we stop at a door that looks precisely the same as dozens of doors we passed on the way. She opens it and orders me to go inside the small, bright room. There is no chair, so I sit on the examining table.

"The priest will be with you shortly," she announces, allowing the door to thud heavily closed, leaving me alone.

Or, I should say, leaving me *mostly* alone.

In moments like these, I can almost hear the gremlin whispering and giggling, though I never see it. When I cover my ears, it only becomes louder.

A tall man, dressed in scrubs with a clerical collar tightly gripping his neck, enters the room. "How are you feeling today, my child?" he asks, in a rich baritone voice.

"Miserable," I admit, but immediately feel the need to soften the statement, "Or, well, slightly miserable. On a scale of one-to-ten, I'm a seven in miserable. Or maybe a three."

"Well, well, well," he says, with a friendly smile, "Let's see if we can get you fixed up. Say 'grace,'" he commands.

"Graaaaaaaaaaaa..." I open my mouth wide as he points a small flashlight to look at my tonsils.

"Very good, you can close."

"...aaaaaaace."

"How long have you experienced the strange disappearance of small, everyday household objects?" he asks, wrapping the blood pressure cuff around my arm.

"My whole life."

"How much water do you drink?" He takes his stethoscope and places the cold metal bell to the center of my forehead, apparently listening to my brainwaves.

"Maybe three glasses a day."

"Do you pause in your hectic and overburdened life to reflect on the majesty of the natural world at least six times a week?" he waves a feather wand—like a cat toy—just in the periphery of my vision. I fail to resist the urge to bat at it with my hands.

"No. No more than two times a week. On a good week."

"Recite the names of the U.S. presidents in chronological order." He holds a large, u-shaped magnet up to my right ear and lets it go. The magnet clatters loudly as it falls to the tile floor.

"George Washington, John Adams, Benjamin Franklin, Franklin Roosevelt, Franklin Franklin..."

"And the names of their wives?" He repeats the magnet test on my left side, with the same result.

"The first one is Martha, then I think they are pretty much all named Jane."

"It's as I thought. You have a severe case of Bogles. The most severe case I've seen."

"What does that even mean?"

He turns to the side table and grabs a pamphlet from a clear-plastic display stand holding up dozens of similar pamphlets. Handing the waxy paper document to me, he continues, "A Bogle is an angry house spirit who exists to create mischief. Clearly one of them attached itself to you."

"So...am I completely screwed?"

"Certainly not. I will personally see to it that we cure you of all your Bogle woes. Go on home, drink a nice big glass of water, reflect on the majesty of the natural world for at least twenty seconds, and I'll be by at eight in the morning to begin the de-Bogling."

"Thank you, doctor."

"Please," he pats my shoulder paternalistically, "I'm not a doctor."

On the bus ride home, I examine my brochure. 'The Truth About Bogles,' read shiny blue letters in a disarming sans-serif font. Below this title is an illustration of a despondent young woman wearing only one shoe while a greenish hand snatches the shoe's pair away behind her back. Staring at the image, I feel a profound sense that, at last, someone understands me.

The second page reveals the grotesque image of a sickly humanoid creature with greasy hair, pointed ears, yellow eyes, and an impossibly wide mouth full of needle-like teeth. "Though rarely seen, Bogles are easily recognizable not only for their unkempt, troll-like appearance, but also for the curving horns extending from their skulls." Shuddering, I try not to imagine this hideous thing in my home, touching my personal belongings.

"Bogles, eh?" A sharp voice draws me from these unhappy reflections.

"It seems there is possibly a Bogle in my home," I respond, looking up. My interlocuter is an elderly man sitting across the aisle from me. His bristly, white mustache undulates as he talks.

"They said my son had a Bogle when he was five," the impressively-mustachioed man continues. "The priest wanted to come over and do a whole de-Bogling process. Fiddle faddle, I says. I got rid of the Bogle myself. All you got to do is show that Bogle who is in charge. Discipline. That's how you drive out those beasts."

I nod, hoping I appear sufficiently grateful for the advice, trying not to be too distracted by the movements of the mustache. My guts churn painfully. Whether my unsettled stomach is caused by the lurching of the bus, the uncanny nature of the old man's facial hair, or the impossible-to-repress mental image of the horned creature hiding my shoe, I cannot tell.

The Bogle turned off my alarm, so the knock of the priest arriving at my apartment awakens me in a full panic. I rush to pull on clothes while opening the front door. There he stands, his immaculate dress and coiffed hair starkly contrasting my dishevelry.

"Ms. Felicity Contentina," he greets me.

"Please come in."

To offer him a seat, I must first move a pile of papers off the armchair, adding them to a nearby stack on the floor. The paper tower leans as precariously as the control I have over my own life.

"The first stage of de-Bogling requires that we use a tempting, sugary treat. Do you have any in the household?"

"I think so, hang on one moment." I leave my guest among the forest of paper piles to rummage through my pantry. In the back, behind the collection of grocery bags that I will eventually remember to take to the recycling center, is a long-forgotten pack of marshmallows. I return to my living room, "Will this work?"

"Yes. Marshmallows are precisely the kind of irresistible temptation we need for the process. What you must do is simply put out a bowl of the sweet treats in your home and let the Bogle gobble them up. Once they are all gone, craving more, the Bogle will leave your home to search for them. When you hear it leave through the front door, throw three drops of holy water on the threshold to seal the portal. Unable to enter the home again, it will be forced to return to the forest caves from whence Bogles originate."

He hands me a vial of holy water.

"That's it? It's so easy!"

"Not as easy as it may sound. For, you see, you must leave the marshmallows out in an easy-to-reach place, but you cannot eat them. If you consume even one marshmallow, the process is ruined and the Bogle will stay."

"No problem! Surely, I can resist a few marshmallows!"

"I certainly hope so," the priest politely and ominously replies, showing himself to the door. "I will return in a week. If the creature is not gone by then, we will escalate the treatment measures."

I am too excited to show him out, as good manners prescribe. Instead, I eagerly grab my largest mixing bowl and dump the entire bag of sugary temptations into it. Shoving stacks of books and old newspapers off my dining table, I place the bowl in easy reach.

"Resist that, Bogle!"

On the third day, the level of marshmallows in the bowl had lowered perceptibly. I try not to pace around the table, since I want the bowl to look unguarded and easy to access. Instead, I spend half the day peering around the corner of the doorway, waiting to catch a glimpse of the monster whose years of terrorizing me are nearly ended. All day, the only thing I can think about is the Bogle and the marshmallows. The delicious marshmallows.

By the sixth day, there are few enough marshmallows that I can easily count them. Only five left. Throughout the day, I take inventory of them. Heading to the closet to grab my jacket before I leave for work—five marshmallows. On my way to the living room to play video games—five marshmallows. Going to the pantry to find an afternoon snack—five marshmallows. Unfortunately, there are zero snacks in the pantry. No doubt, the Bogle ate all of them. That, and I have not remembered to go to the grocery store for weeks.

Walking to the front door to make a grocery run—four marshmallows! The Bogle must have eaten another one! Except... I realize the marshmallow is in my hand. I must have absent-mindedly picked it up when I was walking by. I am very hungry, after all, and there is nothing to eat in the apartment. I lift my hand with every intention of putting the marshmallow back in the bowl. Unfortunately, my willpower fails me.

I eat the fifth marshmallow.

The air-puffed texture and sweet taste linger. Before I know it, the remaining four are in my digestive tract. I feel satiated and ashamed.

It might all work out. Maybe the Bogle will leave now that the marshmallows are gone. I listen for the thud of the door, ready with my small vial of holy water. The thud never comes. After hours...or at least fifteen minutes...of waiting, I despair. In my guilt and disappointment, I do the only thing I can--I go to the corner store and buy myself a new bag of marshmallows. They were delicious, and now I need some comfort food to cheer me up.

The priest communicates his disappointment in me with a grave, stereotypically priest-like shake of his head as I detail the failure of the marshmallow plan. "My child, that was the *easy* way to rid yourself of this curse."

"Can we try again? I will do better. I won't eat the marshmallows a second time!"

"No trick ever works twice on a Bogle. We must increase the intensity of our curative efforts," he projects, as though on a pulpit, his voice overwhelming my small apartment. "It is time for the SBF."

"Like sunscreen?"

"No. That's SPF. This is the Standardized Bogle Form."

I must not seem appropriately impressed, because he clearly sees the need to launch into a lecture. "You see, every Bogle is as unique as the human it torments. As such, different Bogles require different solutions. Bogles are very resistant to anti-Bogle measures, so it is imperative that we do not build up its defenses by wasting time on ineffective solutions. This form, or, I should say, series of forms, help us identify what curative methods will be most effective against a specific Bogle. The forms will begin with a series of questions about..."

At this point, I am afraid to admit, I stop paying complete attention. I continue to nod encouragingly to the very long explanation, but cannot really make meaning of his words. Instead, I idly glance out the window at my series of dead and dying potted plants. A few weeks ago, the Bogle stole my watering can, so the innocent flowers were parched for several weeks. Then, when I finally remembered to buy a new one, I was probably a little overzealous in my watering efforts, trying to make up for the period of drought. I am just making a mental note that the begonias look particularly unsalvageable, when I realize the priest is finishing his thesis. I revert to listening just in time to hear his summary.

"In short, it is an assessment that you need to complete to identify which technique will be most effective in evicting your individual Bogle."

"Okay," I respond, hoping I sound like I know what he is talking about.

He takes a stack of papers, at least a foot tall, out of his bag and plunks them on my coffee table next to my existing stacks of papers. "I will return in a week to collect the form. Then we will be rid of your Bogle."

A week? To climb this mountain of questions with my pen? But what other choice do I have? It is this or I will be stuck with my tormentor for the rest of my life. I collapse into a seated position on the floor to begin the impossible task. The priest also left a box of pens, which is a blessing, because my Bogle took all the writing utensils away. I begin filling out the first few fields—my name, address, and favorite flavor of shaved ice—as the priest shows himself, once again, to the door.

Each day I write long into the night until I collapse atop the paper pile. Early each noon I awaken and, with only a cup of coffee to sustain me, resume the unpreferable assignment. My hand cramps, my eyes glaze over, my mind numbs, yet I answer question after question. *At what age did I first talk? What were the names and astrological signs of the doctor and nurses who delivered me? When I go out to eat with my friends, am I the friend designated to eat any unwanted free pickle spears? How many words can I create from the letters used to write 'undis-*

ciplined'? *What is the primary export of Bulgaria? What was the cultural significance of pet rocks?*

I stop wondering what any of these questions have to do with Bogles, let alone my own personal Bogle. I am merely answering. Forever. Was there a time before the form? I cannot remember. I have always been and will always be trapped in this purgatory of filling out forms.

Until, at last—sweet mercy!—I reach the final page. Only one question left: *What do you want to be when you grow up?*

I hesitate. That is a difficult one to answer. Glancing at the calendar, I confirm there are still two whole days until the priest's return. So, there is no rush. I have plenty of time to answer the question. After days of tortuous surveying, I am only one question away from being done—done with forms and done with Bogles. I deserve a little break before answering this final question. Besides, I need time to decide if I would rather be a blacksmith using period-accurate tools in a living history museum or an online dating profile ghostwriter.

When I hear the knock on my door, pulling my mind out of the disjointed world of dreams to the equally disjointed world of my own apartment, I realize immediately that I never wrote my last answer for the Bogle survey. Messily pulling an old band sweatshirt over my head and opening the door, I hope the priest will give me a minute to write my answer, which will, of course, be disc jockey.

"Did you complete the SBF?"

"Yes. Mostly. I only have one question left! Then you can review my answers and determine which de-Bogling method we should use."

He covers his face with his hands in a manner that communicates I already messed something up. Again.

"There isn't a problem, right? It will only take me one second to write 'disc jockey,'" I assure him, feeling a panic rising inside my chest, rushing over to the table to try to find one of the dozen pens that were there in the box just a few days before.

"No, it will not work," he sighs.

The Bogle hid all the pens.

"What do you mean? I completed the forms. There are hundreds of pages here, all filled out, see?" My frantic stammering mirrors the frantic motions of my hands as I grasp for a pen on, under, beside, or anywhere near the table.

"That is not how the form works."

At last, I realize there is a pen shoved into my sports bra. Without even blushing, I reach into my shirt and pull it out, swiftly jotting 'DJ' down on the page. For a second, I am tempted to dash it out and write 'roller coaster engineer' instead, but I resist the urge.

"See? It's done!" I assure him.

"It's too late. The forms themselves are what drives the Bogle away. The story about them helping me determine a method was all a fib. Bogles find forms so tedious that they are driven out by the sheer boredom of completing them. However, since you did not complete the form in a week, this cure will not work."

"That's not fair! You lied to me about what the form was!"

"Lord forgive me, yes, I lied. But that is standard de-Bogling procedure. If I told you the true nature of the form, it would not have worked. The Bogle can hear everything we say, and it would know why you were filling out the forms, putting it on its guard. That and, honestly, if I told you the purpose of the form was to be boring, you most likely would have been too bored to complete it."

I am incensed at the injustice of being lied to, but I agree with him about me being unlikely to fill out the forms if I knew they were supposed to be boring. "What do we do now?"

"There is but one option remaining to us. I hoped to avoid this," He pauses, taking a deep and dramatic breath before announcing, "We must exorcise the evil being from your home."

Predictably, I gasp.

"Prepare yourself for great suffering," he continues, "as the exorcism is an unpleasant experience for the Bogle host."

"I'm ready. I'll do anything to be rid of this monster!"

From his satchel he takes two crucifixes and one bag of jalapeño-flavored potato chips with the words "extra spicy" emblazoned threateningly on the front. He keeps one crucifix while handing me the other and the chips.

"When I give the signal, you must eat the chips. No matter how spicy, you must not drink water! No matter how flamin' hot, you must not alleviate the pain with even a drop of milk!"

Shivering at these words, I steel myself and assure him, "I am ready."

"Repeat after me," he says, holding his crucifix high, "Sower of chaos, we reject you!"

Mimicking his motions, and doing my level best to repeat his words verbatim, I reply, "Sewer...oh, wait, was it 'sower'?—of chaos, we reject you!"

Inside my 600-square-foot apartment, I feel a breeze pick up, though I know the windows are closed and the A/C has not worked properly in months.

"Maker of mischief, we despise you!"

"Mischief maker, we really dislike you!"

A dark cloud rises all around us, obscuring the priest's face. I worry that I accidentally left the oven on. I cling tightly to the crucifix and the bag of chips as the wind rises to the levels of a gale and threatens to blow them out of my hand.

"Go on, get!"

"Go on, get!"

The smoke swirls in swift circles. The sound is deafening, like that of a rapidly approaching train. I feel as though my feet are rising off my carpeted floor. One thought echoes through the cavern of my mind, *this exorcism is the real deal!*

"Bogle begone!"

"Bogle begone!"

I can barely hear the shouts above the storm, "Contentina, eat the chips! Eat the spicy potato chips *now!*"

Plunging one end of the crucifix into the low-density polyethylene film, I pop open the bag and shovel spicy chips into my mouth. The jalapeño flavor is like fire to my mid-western palette, but I continue eating them through tears. At last, my fingers grasp the final oily crumbs. As I place them on my tongue, the entire room returns to normal as quick as it takes me to burp. The wind and smoke blink out of existence. All that remains is me, the priest, and my many piles of papers, still leaning precariously, undisturbed by the storm's onslaught.

"Here." The priest opens a carton of milk, handing it to me.

Still gasping through the peppery pain, I shake my head resolutely.

He grins proudly at me, announcing, "You passed your final test."

My eyelids flutter and my knees quake.

"My child, you are exhausted. Go and rest. When you awaken tomorrow, the Bogle will be gone and you can begin your life unencumbered with misplaced cellular phones and other petty travails. It is impossible for the Bogle to remain in this place now."

I stumble to my bed, tears wetting my cheeks. Tears from the heat of the chips, yes, but also tears from joy. I hardly hear the priest murmur, "I'll have my front desk team send you the bill," as he gently closes the front door behind him. I am asleep before my head hits the mattress where there would normally be a pillow except the Bogle pushed it onto the floor.

Cold. Cold and hard.

I waken, shivering, on an uncomfortable surface, my back aching as though I were sleeping on concrete. Wait. My palms register the sensation of the substrate below me. I *am* sleeping on concrete. Disoriented, I try to blink meaning into what I see. I am lying in the parking lot outside my apartment.

The Bogle must have kicked me out! *Of my own home!*

Furious, I race up the stairs to my door. Finding it locked, I pound on the wood, "Let me in! Let me in, you meanie!"

Peering through the window, it is difficult to see into the living room that is obscured by the reflection from street lights. I can barely make out a silhouette moving about. Screaming in desperation, I grab my pot of long-dead begonias and smash it through the glass. Rushing through the break, I burst inside. A shadow flees down the hall. I rush after it, finding myself in the closet. A grasp for it, only to find there is nothing here. A thump from behind me spurs me to turn and run the seven steps to my bathroom. There! I see it! Nearly invisible in the darkness, I perceive the outline of something in front of me. With a triumphant, "Got you!" I flip the switch, pouring piercing bright light into the cramped room.

Yellow eyes and a grin of needle-like teeth pin me like a beetle in a display case. The Bogle is not physically standing in the room. Far worse, it is in the mirror. It is my reflection, staring wide-eyed at me. It wears the same wrinkled No Doubt 2004 tour sweatshirt I fell asleep in. It blinks in perfect time with my own blinking. I notice twisting horns emerge from its forehead in a grotesque salute to the heavens. Moving slowly, like a predator try not to startle its prey, my hands—and the reflection's hands—reach up to my own forehead until I feel the texture of the horns atop my own skull. I watch in horror as the Bogle and I open our mouths wide to let out a single, terrified scream.

I no longer fight the Bogle. We live in relative peace, these days. Of course, it still hides an occasional shoe from me, the little scamp. I buy us marshmallows to snack on and make a point to reflect on the sheer majesty of the natural world a little more often than I once did. For the most part, me and my Bugaboo—that's what I call it—are content sharing our existence, spending our days working down at the living history museum and writing screenplays for a science-fiction murder mystery in the evenings. It is a beautiful, if a bit messy, life.

Jessica Feather (she/her) followed her love of language until it led her to a BA in Linguistics at the University of Texas. During the day she works as a grant writer for hire and in her free time she creates short pieces of fantasy, horror, and dark comedy. Discovering that she had ADHD when she was in her mid-30s was like solving a life-long mystery about herself--revealing the secrets to her many struggles and strengths. Jessica lives in Santa Fe, New Mexico, with her husband, dog, cat, and surprisingly tall axolotl.

NELLY'S WORLD

ARTHUR H. MANNERS

Rachel had been buried less than four hours before Nelly escaped upstairs to her gaming rig. After the stragglers headed home from the wake, I stood in her bedroom doorway. The house was silent except for the *click-clack* of her joysticks.

Nelly's preteen body slumped against the rig's contours, which were shaped like an ebony-black, hollowed-out egg. The heavy visor covered her eyes and pimply forehead, and her hands melded with the button-laced joysticks embedded in the armrests. As she played *Frontiers*, her favorite game, transparent haptic memory-gel oozed around her body until only her hands and face remained uncovered.

Losing my wife had hit me like a freight train, but I saw no signs of pain on Nelly's face, no tears. Where did she go in there? What could so effectively insulate her from losing her mother?

"Everyone's gone home now, Nell. Come and eat," I said.

She didn't respond, spinning the joysticks. The rig pivoted a little on its gyroscopic axis, indicating that, wherever she was, she was moving at great speed.

It was odd to see the gel cradle her. Nelly had always cringed from skin-on-skin contact. I hadn't held her in ten years, since she was old enough to crawl away from me.

"I put aside some food. Nobody's touched it. Chicken tenders and peas, with extra ketchup." One of the meals from her short list of acceptable fare. "Come on, there's nobody around."

I took a step into the room, the agreed symbol for *enough is enough*. The haptic gel retreated into the rig's innards, and the seat swung upright to deposit her on the carpet. We looked at one another, and I knew that I was supposed to say something comforting.

I'll take care of you. It'll be okay. We'll get through this.

But fresh pain pounded in my chest, cutting off contact between my body and my brain.

Nelly turned on the hallway light as she shuffled off downstairs, illuminating the mess that had been half-hidden by the gloom. I cringed at the abandoned heaps of dirty clothes, empty chocolate wrappers, clusters of glasses of flat coke. The room smelled of mold and stale sweat. Even with the live-in nurse helping, I hadn't been able to keep up with the cleaning while taking care of Rachel.

Stung by the sight of the mess, I picked up Nell's headset and glanced inside at the display: the antiquated graphics of *Frontiers*, on pause. The complexity of the menu startled me.

Most other games had inbuilt AIs these days, anticipating what a player wanted and serving it up to them before they were consciously aware of it. *Frontiers* was much older, a bare-bones crafting game advertised as being infinitely configurable — Minecraft reimagined by the world's worst pedant. It was notorious for its complexity and cumbersome interface, by all accounts a chore to play. When I had first bought the game, I had quickly written it off as a needlessly intricate sandbox.

I couldn't remember how to even unpause the game, let alone look around. I heard Nelly coming and hastily put the visor back where I found it.

"We need to get you something else to do, Nell. I'm sorry that I haven't had much time for you since Mum got sick. But now..." My throat clamped shut and I struggled for a moment. "Drawing. Drawing is good. I used to draw all the time when I was your age.

Much better for your brain than whatever they're piping into that rig."

Nelly didn't answer me. The only things she ever said to me were "Can I have a snack?" or "Can I play *Frontiers*?" When Rachel forced Nelly to write me birthday cards, she had addressed me as Jack instead of Dad. But somehow, I really thought that in that moment she might burst into hot fat tears and come running into my arms.

I was embarrassed by the strength of that fantasy, how much I needed it.

But Nelly simply brushed by me, carrying a plate of chicken tenders. I noticed that half the peas were missing, probably strewn all over the stairs. In moments she had wolfed her food and returned to *Frontiers*, leaving me alone in the room.

The curtains were drawn, leaving only an inch gap for the intrusion of a few spears of dusty sunlight. It was my daily ritual to stride into the room to throw the curtains open, as though the act might turn Nelly into a normal girl who spoke full sentences and lived in the real world and cared about her sick mother. But today the sunlight seemed to mock me. I couldn't imagine how the sun could go on, warming skin and nourishing life. Didn't the world know what I had lost?

Except for the *click-clack* of the joysticks on Nelly's rig, the room was as silent as the rest of the house. That silence had reigned over the wake for hours, until the final stragglers fled. The whole thing had been a sorry sight: fifty people crammed into our living room and lean-to extension, eating limp catering that all smelled vaguely of a three-day-old gym bag.

Rachel deserved a better send-off than that.

Nelly had managed only a few minutes downstairs after the first guests arrived, before she slunk away to sit on the stairs with her head buried between her knees. I did my best to smooth things over while friends and family tried not to look at her askance over their sausage rolls.

Her desperation to get upstairs and play hung over the day like a heavy shawl. I felt it snag at my every effort to give the ordeal a shred of dignity. Now, she jerked the joysticks violently in all directions, her fingers a blur on the embedded buttons and spinners.

A childish part of me wished she could at least pretend to be upset, force herself to shed a single tear. Show in some way that she noticed Rachel's absence.

The rig's gel had grown up around her black funeral dress. I hadn't noticed the big rip running down one side. Seeing it made me feel exhausted. All I had asked was that she sit still during the service —I knew she found it difficult, but she could have tried, just once, for me. Instead, she had shuffled her knee all day, filling the church with the swishing of polyester.

Looking at the dress, my patience frayed, then snapped.

"What's so important in there that it couldn't wait a day? Even a few minutes," I hissed.

Nelly paused and pushed up her visor, peering at me with watchful confusion.

All the fight drained out of me. I always felt like such a bully when I confronted her. Humiliated, I avoided her gaze, glancing along the tabletop. I noticed that Nelly had taken one of the red petunias we draped over Rachel's casket.

"You took a flower from mummy's service? That's, uh, that's nice, honey. That's good. She'd have liked that." I didn't know who I was trying to convince. I fled the room, hiding my face with my wrist. "Put it in water or it'll die, okay?"

I spent the day cleaning up, trying and failing to remember where Rachel had kept everything. The house seemed to thrum with silence, so much that the rig's *click-clacking* seemed deafening.

Frontiers was going to be a problem. With Rachel gone, I needed to focus on Nelly's wellbeing. We needed to eat right, get some sunlight, process our grief, reconnect. At least, that's what the internet said.

If I stood a chance of keeping Nelly out of that rig, I had to know where she was going—what was so worth ignoring reality for. I went to my computer and accessed the network logs. She had been in a single *Frontiers* session all year. Glancing over my shoulder, I used my admin privileges to join the session.

An endless grassy field under a blue sky appeared on the screen. In the distance stood a single mountain, so high it vanished into a haze. Without the visor and chair, the game was hopelessly clunky. After a lot of grabbing at nothing and jumping in place, I found the key to walk forward.

After minutes, nothing seemed to change. I held down the key.

Between bouts of walking in a straight line, I experimented with the controls, but struggled to map my keystrokes to any resulting actions. It took almost an hour before, without warning, my avatar crested a rise, and I spotted Nelly.

Her hands were lost in a cloud of rainbow-colored tendrils. Her brow was creased with concentration. After a minute something emerged from the cloud and shot away up the mountainside. I glimpsed wood, nails, a triangular pane of glass. Nell watched it go, then resumed her work. By the fifth time an object emerged from the cloud, I guessed that she was crafting pieces of a building.

My mind reeled. I had mashed the keyboard hundreds of times to no coherent effect. How was she doing that?

Eventually a last block zipped away, and the cloud dissolved. Nelly gave a casual flick of her heel and flew away in pursuit of her creations.

There was no way for me to follow. I logged off and sat staring at the black screen.

I looked up the game wiki, hoping for a quick tutorial. Instead, I found tens of thousands of pages of documentation, managed by a cult following of only a few dozen people. When I looked for controls on crafting materials, I found not keystrokes, but equations.

Knowing me, I'd need a calculator and a Bunsen burner to craft a simple, untextured cube. But Nelly had been crafting photo-real materials. I had seen *grit* on that window.

And apparently, she could fly. There was nothing in the wiki about that at all.

The whole thing was clearly a waste of time. But I had to admit that whatever she was doing was mentally demanding. All I had to offer outside *Frontiers* was a few crayons. I shuddered to think of the tantrum if I pulled her away from the game without something to keep her occupied.

Over the next few days my head rang with muttered condolences. *Rachel was such a treasure. Taken from us too soon. You'll get through it, Jack. Just take it one day at a time.*

All of it mixed with Rachel's pleading. *Nelly's every bit as normal as you and me. She just plays by different rules. No loud noises. No touching. Stick to the rules. It's not asking for much.*

I scrambled for routine, but gravity seemed stronger now—an overwhelming impetus to sink to the floor and stay there. I slouched in front of the TV for endless hours. It wasn't enough; I found myself playing mobile phone games at the same time, holding the screen inches from my nose, slicing cascades of virtual lemons and grapefruit. I was hiding from the world just like Nelly, from the silence of our home and the gaping hole in my life. Most of all, I hid from the fact that I could barely remember what things had been like when Rachel had been healthy.

A knot of fear blossomed in the pit of my stomach. Was this how it was going to be from now on? I had never learned how to talk to Nelly. Rach had been the one who reacted when the doctors gave us Nelly's diagnosis, had bought all the books and signed us up to night classes.

From upstairs came the same incessant noise.

Click-click-clack.

Frontiers. Always that same pointless, impossible game.

At night, I stood in Nelly's bedroom doorway, watching her play. The cartoon elephants painted on the wall grinned in mockery. They were the reason we stopped calling her Isabel and started calling her Nelly. Rachel had paraded her around on her shoulders, singing *Nelly the elephant packed her trunk and said goodbye to the circus!*

Nelly squealed if anyone else touched her, including me, but Rach had that way with her. She spoke about another person inside Nelly, who was creative and kind and funny, but spoke a language nobody else knew.

Rach had always been an optimist like that. I loved my daughter, but I had never seen that other person; I couldn't imagine anyone surviving such a prison.

Even after several doctors gave the same diagnosis, I had rejected it. We were going to be rockstar parents, raise a well-adjusted, self-actualized young woman. Charismatic, tough as nails, with a wicked sense of humor.

I had dyslexia as a child, but my parents hadn't lowered their expectations, even if once or twice it meant beating the spelling into me. This was no different.

But it didn't go that way. Instead, we woke every day to fix Nelly's pills and make the same meals. I went to the office, and Rachel took Nelly to school, working from a nearby cafe in case Nelly had a meltdown. Rachel would try to play with her in the evenings, but Nelly couldn't deal with skin-on-skin contact. Once she was old enough, she disappeared upstairs every night to play *Frontiers*.

The game had stolen her from us.

Clack-clack-click.

Nelly seemed to sink only deeper into the game. I worried that she might vanish into it altogether. I couldn't risk her health going downhill. How had Rach charmed her?

I didn't remember. I remembered so little of our life together. I spent long nights thinking on it, but I kept coming back to that simple horror. At some point, I had surrounded myself with a carapace of work, food, TV marathons, *uh huhs* and *yes honeys*.

I had to find a way to fix things, no matter how ugly things got.

Rach had treated Nell like glass, but she could handle a little tough love. Her condition wasn't as bad as some kids at her school—though Rach was always telling me there were no conditions. *Just words made up to spotlight people who don't fit in to a world designed for minds like ours.*

Whatever that meant. Life was hard for everyone, and everyone had to adjust.

My sister came to visit. Like me, she never knew how to act around Nelly. We drank tea while looking in at her playing *Frontiers.* "Jack, it isn't my place, but look at her. How are you going to get her to stop?" she said.

I didn't have an answer. But only days later, Nelly sat on *Frontiers* for twelve straight hours. After she ignored countless instructions to wrap up, I shut down the home network.

Bad mistake. She started screaming before I could begin to explain.

"Nell, stop it. Time's up!"

She scratched me. She bit her nails a lot, and the jagged edges sliced the back of my hand like a cheese grater. She bared her teeth, and I thought she was about to bite me, but then I realized why she was making that face.

I released her wrist, which had grown pale from my grip. "I'm sorry, Nell. Please, don't do that. It's okay, I'm here." I kissed her clammy palms, but she recoiled.

I stood to leave and caught a glimpse through her visor: a grass-covered mountainside, golden sunlight, patches of red. Beside the visor lay the petunia from the funeral, limp and sad. Nell hadn't put it in water.

I retreated before she could explode again and checked the *Frontiers* session from my PC. Nothing seemed different, but she had been in-game for hundreds of hours, and I had seen what she could do with a few minutes. I itched to know what could shield her from the pain of losing Rachel — I couldn't help but crave that same oblivion.

For the next few days, I let the routine continue, studying her. Nell slept, ate, and played *Frontiers.* When she wasn't playing, she stared at the dying flower on her desk. I implored her to put it in water.

I worked when I could, handled condolence cards, and made meals. And now I played *Frontiers* too. It took me a week to go fifty meters up the mountainside, and I felt every step of the climb. Not in aching legs but in throbbing fingers, as I stabbed the keys over and over. I scoured the net for a workaround and came up with nothing. *Frontiers* offered no shortcuts.

The steep rock-face diverged into passages that split further into some kind of maze. My mind reeled: she had the capacity to make a three-dimensional puzzle in a game so complicated that I could barely walk in a straight line.

After the maze came a tunnel filled with traps. Then false floors, revolving walls. Beyond that lay a gorge a mile deep with an invisible bridge and a dark shadow that followed me.

I didn't know much of *Frontiers*, but I knew enough to be certain these were not standard features. She had designed all this. Despite myself, I became intrigued, maybe even a little addicted. She had no idea I was there, but it almost felt like getting to know her.

Then we would eat together, or I would try to strike up a conversation, and she was the same old Nelly. The obstacles in the game almost seemed to beckon me forward, yet she couldn't bear my attention in the physical world.

Frontiers kept me busy in the day, but I had the same dream every night: the time we told Nelly about Rach's leukemia. Nelly had refused to look in our direction, even when we used the buzzword that meant she had to make eye contact. Then she asked for a Twix.

I knew it wasn't her fault, but I couldn't handle how much it hurt Rach. I never admitted it, but while I shepherded Rach to ward after ward, something cancerous also grew in me.

All that had to stop. I had to break down the wall between us.

I gathered my courage and went to Nelly's room. Maybe if I asked her about the world she had built, she would open up.

Then I saw the petunia, still on her desk. A thousand times I had seen her staring at it as it mummified. All I had asked is that she put it in water—to not add to the number of things that wilted to nothing in our home.

My good intentions flash boiled. I bolted into the room and ripped the power cord from the wall. The rig sighed and became an inanimate lump of metal and plastic. Nelly sat motionless for a moment, then pushed off the visor.

I went to her, but she scratched at me. She screeched, making my ears ring.

"No, Nelly. You don't get to do this. Stop it right now!"

We struggled until she wriggled out of the chair and we both fell to the floor.

"You were everything to her!" I yelled. "Why couldn't you have cared when she went away?"

Nelly screamed so hard that the tendons in her neck threatened to break the skin. I scrambled away. She continued to buck and flail and pull her hair. Not a tantrum, but the desperate wail of a person on fire.

I ran, stumbling through the house, knocking things over. I went to the computer, caught the monitor with the flat of my palm and sent it crashing into the wall. I staggered to the bedroom and fell face-first onto the bed.

Nelly ran away some time in the night.

I had made a peace offering of pancakes drowned in maple syrup, a forbidden favorite. But when ten minutes of coaxing received no response, I went to her bedroom and found it empty. Her school bag was gone, along with stuffed toys, headphones, and the desiccated petunia.

I drove around the neighborhood in a panic. This wasn't the first time Nelly had run away, but it had been Rach who had the knack for knowing where she might go.

I called my sister and regretted it; she insisted on sitting in the car with me. It didn't take long for us to start yelling at one another. We drove all over town, posted on social media, and put in a report with the police.

We kept going into the night. In the morning my sister left to go to work, promising to come back later. I kept driving until I started seeing double, then headed home. I made a pot of strong coffee and ate some crackers. My head was pounding and my mouth was dry as sand.

I stood in the hallway and stared into Nelly's bedroom. The silence of the house skulked at my heels. Fighting the urge to find relief in a bottle of whisky, I entered the room and collapsed into the rig. I touched the impressions that Nelly's wrists had made in the armrests. Desperate for some clue, I slipped on the visor and, after a brief hesitation over the haptic gel, logged in using Nelly's account.

For all I could tell, I was now standing on a steep mountainside. The view was like nothing reality could offer: the plain lay miles below, running to an impossible horizon thousands of miles away. The wind licked at my skin, and the activation of all my senses did what my computer monitor could not: reminded me of a family holiday to the beach in Devon. Nelly had been in her lazy phase, big enough to walk yet insistent on being carried. Rach had suffered aching shoulders and we'd bickered about it for most of the trip.

But there had been ten minutes when we stood in the dunes with the evening breeze tickling our sunburned skin. The shape of the dunes split the airflow into turbulent eddies, giving a peculiar feeling, like caresses from the hands of ocean sprites. The similarity of the sensations was uncanny.

But Nelly had been too young to remember such things.

I began to ascend. The mountaintop was still far away; I could only make out the outline of a structure, and a column of smoke. The ground was carpeted with red flowers, leading up in tiered terraces. I was so focused on reaching the peak that it took me a few minutes to realize what they were.

Petunias. I looked around at the endless copies, pristine and heavy with dew, perfect to the smallest detail.

I gripped the rock but a sense of falling persisted. I had felt such rage when Nelly watched the petunia on her desk fade away. But she had made countless more in here, and in here they would never die.

I started walking again, but the shock of brilliant red was inescapable. I broke into a run, almost fell from the terrace. I itched to tear the visor from my head and reach for that whiskey. Anything was better than those velvet-smooth petals, than knowing how much time and effort it had taken to craft them.

But then I reached the mountain peak and all thought was obliterated. When seen from above, the terraces, gorges and the plain much farther below formed a collage. All of it, a single titanic flower.

I had only experienced something similar at the Grand Canyon: something inside me stilled by its sheer enormity. I had the disturbing impression that I couldn't have rivalled this if I spent a hundred years in the game.

I spun away from it. It was only because I was already reeling that I didn't cry out the moment I saw what lay nearby.

The house perched on the summit like it belonged there, pine-clad and rickety and smelling of the sea. A mote of the mundane in an impossible place.

For a few vertigo-stricken moments I saw two houses: this glaring anomaly and the real house, as it had been, in those far-distant woods. A doomed camping trip to the Forest of Dean. We had stumbled on it in a glade while trying to calm Nelly, who couldn't handle the tent or the sleeping bag or anything to do with camping. But when we walked into that house, she had gone quiet. We ate a cheap lunch from a plastic bag while sitting under the crumbling eaves.

I ran my hand over the cladding; paint peeling from the sun, wood made brittle by salt. My memory of the real thing felt like a dream, dredged up from the sludge of a neglected decade. We had eaten limp sandwiches and gotten sticky hands from spilled lemonade. There were spiders and broken bottles and cigarette butts.

But we had giggled ourselves giddy. I couldn't remember what had been so funny, and the absence of that knowledge stabbed at me. Perhaps it had been some secret that could have made all the other days better, if only we had been able to preserve it.

I went inside and found that the house had more rooms than its real-world twin.

In one room lay the detritus of childhood memories: a favorite red ball, years of train tickets, a doll that had been left in a hotel by accident, the dining table from our old house.

The next room was warm. It took me a minute to realize the warmth wasn't in the air but under my skin. Something I recognized by instinct; embryonic, timeless, nameless.

One room was filled with my own voice, overheard mean-spirited mutterings that filled my gut with shame.

One was filled with Twix bars from floor to ceiling, which made me laugh out loud.

The last room housed Rach's laugh, which danced in the rafters and broke the last of me.

Dazed, I fled the house. Outside, I found a burning pyre. It hovered mid-air, a few feet beyond the cliff edge. The fire burned so hot it was almost white. On top lay a body, obscured by the flames but unmistakable in profile. By some optical illusion, the pyre seemed to be receding into open blue skies, though it never got any farther from the cliff. The overall effect was of a burning boat, floating endlessly out to sea.

I recoiled as another memory surfaced. A long weekend at Lyme Regis under a grim sky. The hotel could have been called second-rate by somebody in a charitable mood, but they had served good wine. Rach and I had been singing by sunset, and we'd pinched an extra bottle and staggered with Nelly down to the beachfront.

Delirious at the reprieve from doctors and support groups, we fell about and played silly games. We ended up sitting on the sea wall as the sun ducked below the waves.

"I've always wanted a Viking funeral," Rach said. It would be years before she would hear the diagnosis, but in my jumbled memory her expression was touched with terrible knowing.

She waved the bottle and sank into the sand, slurring, "Don't let me molder underground or sit in an urn. Put me to sea."

Nell had promised. That made me mad because we worked so

hard not to confuse her. It had been drunken nonsense. A fantasy of being freed from responsibility. Until this moment, like so much else, I had treated it like something to endure and forget.

But someone had remembered everything.

Drunk or not, Rach would have preferred this a thousand times over what I have given her: a cheap plot by the hedges and an awkward wake filled with people I barely knew. I thought I was alone, but the rawness and fury and desolation inside me was painted all over this mountain.

When I had the strength to stand, I took off the visor. I slunk downstairs and found Nelly in the living room, watching TV. Relief and shame washed over me—she was home and safe, but she must have also seen me in the chair, known what I had been doing.

I joined her on the sofa and we watched TV in silence. I waited for her anger, but it never came.

Later, I made dinner and then we went to bed. It took me a whole day to work up the courage to break the stalemate. I made tenders and fries for dinner with ice cream for dessert. Then, I joined her in *Frontiers*.

I took my time, crossed the wastelands, climbed the mountain. This time there were no traps, no puzzles. She watched my progress from the peak. Sometime in the early hours of the morning I reached the pyre. We stood side by side watching the flames.

"I miss her too," I said.

Arthur H. Manners is a British author of speculative fiction. He has lived with daily anxiety for many years; while he's high functioning most of the time, debilitating episodes of severe anxiety and subsequent burnout have shaped the trajectory of his life. "Nelly's World" was inspired by these experiences, and experiences shared by close friends and family on the neurodivergent spectrum.

Arthur's work is published/forthcoming in places like Dreamforge Anvil, Drabblecast, and Writers of the Future Vol. 39. He has a background in physics and data science, and lives near Cambridge with his partner and their cat, Rolo. He sometimes fails at social media on Twitter (@a_h_manners) and Instagram (docmanners). Find his website and newsletter over at arthurmanners.com.

EDITOR'S NOTE

Thank you again for reading *Divergent Realms: Science Fiction and Fantasy Stories About Neurodivergence*. I hope you enjoyed it. Please consider leaving a review on Amazon or Goodreads. Reviews are very helpful, as they help other readers in deciding whether to buy the book or not.

As I stated in the foreword, beyond providing entertainment, the goal of this book is to expand neurodiversity representation in fiction. My hope is to eventually see more opportunities in the field for neurodivergent writers and to see more publishers creating neurodiverse content. However, I cannot change a whole industry by myself. If you believe this goal to be worthwhile, you can help by sharing or talking about this book on social media or wherever else you see fit.

Lastly, consider joining my mailing list at subscribepage.io/5izRKR. You'll receive a FREE story for signing up, and you'll receive updates about my latest projects.

ACKNOWLEDGMENTS

In addition to the fourteen authors whose stories are featured in this anthology, there are some others whom I'd like to thank for their aid in bringing this together. First is my wife, Jamie Odell, for assisting me in the editing process and for being there for me through all the challenges I've faced in the last few years. I think it is no exaggeration to say that without her constant love and support, I would not have been able to put something like this together. Next, I would like to thank my family, who have likewise been a great help to me through these challenging years. It is thanks to the financial generosity of my parents, Doug and Wynne Odell, that I was able to pay these authors a rate they deserve, as well as hire a first-rate team to assist in various aspects of publishing and marketing. That brings me to Melissa Dalton Martinez, owner of The Book Break, and her staff, whose services have been invaluable for getting me through the parts of this process I stink at (which is most of them). Lastly, I would like to thank my closest friends, who are not unlike family themselves. Several of my autistic friends, in particular, helped me learn at an early age that I was not alone in my weirdness, and that there were others out there who were like me. They taught me to embrace and accept myself for who I am, and that's worth everything in the world.

ABOUT THE EDITOR

Riley Odell is an autism and neurodiversity advocate and a writer of horror, comedy, and bizarro which explores the absurdity of the human condition. He lives in Fort Collins, Colorado with his wife Jamie and their two pet children. Their daughter is Sadie, a dog, and their son is Newton, a rabbit. In addition to writing, Riley enjoys reading, video games, and eating cheese. This is his first time ever attempting the creation of an anthology, but it may not be his last. Find out more at rileyodellwriter.com or on Facebook at facebook.com/rileyodellauthor.